The Old Red Chair

And its Secrets

M Y Parker

Mark Your Text Publishing
markyourtext.com

First published in the UK in 2022
By Mark Your Text
Copyright © May Parker 2022

Cover design by Sadie Butterworth-Jones

A CIP catalogue record for this book is available from
the British Library

ISBN: 978-0-9559075-5-5

Dedicated to my newly found and beautiful niece
Emma D

"I could not have supposed a niece would ever have
been so much to me

Jane Austen

"Omnia vincit amor: et nos cedamus amori"

Virgil Ecl. 10.69

"Love conquers all: let us too yield to love"

Chapter One

Grandma

August 2019

Heavy rain pelting the window pane was the only sound in the room.

Dave squinted as his curse simultaneously reverberated across the glass. The road beyond the privet hedge remained empty of traffic. He turned to face the darkened space reminding himself this would be the last time he could take in the view he loved. He scanned the room full of china ornaments, photos, books and memories, allowing his mind to wander back to the days when, as a small boy, he sat at his grandmother's feet engrossed in the stories she read to him. He remembered her clever intonations which brought stories to life and allowed him to see and hear the many characters she enacted so well. He walked over to the alcove shelf set to one side of the brick fireplace and gently ran his fingers across the spines of books and his heart suddenly felt heavier as his eyes fell on children's story books he remembered, in particular the Roger Hargreaves 'Mr Men' series. He gently eased out 'Mr Tickle', his favourite character, and was uplifted at the memory of his Grandma having to read it to him over and over and over again.

He smiled as he crossed the room to the old settee with its now discoloured burgundy coloured fabric and well squashed cushions, and found himself drawn to the once vibrant, red armchair. Stroking its now faded arms he gently eased himself into the sagging cushion seat. Closing his eyes he was immediately transported to the day of his grandmother's eightieth birthday. She was a bit drunk if truth be told and her natural humour and put-downs kept friends and family amused, especially as the more Champagne she drank the more risqué her jokes became. He laughed aloud as he recalled her saying she never liked her name and when she was young asked her father why she was called Emma and not Rose like her very, very best friend Rose Dean. *'Right bloody rose you'll be when you're eighty and wrinkled'* she remembered him saying, *'and he was right'* she laughed, *'look at me now, I'm eighty and you could screw me into a ceiling socket head first; definitely not a rose!'*

A petite lady wearing her auburn hair in a bun at the nape of her neck and always smartly dressed, Emma was the epitome of style. Dave often wondered where his 6ft height came from as his Mother Sara and Grandmother Emma were only five foot two, although his grandmother insisted she was five foot two and three quarters. He couldn't remember ever seeing a photograph of his father so didn't know if he was tall too, or whether he favoured him in other ways like his blonde hair and dark blue eyes.

From the age of four when cared for by his grandmother Dave knew his parents died in a traffic accident. In time he accepted this traumatic change in his young life and channelled all his love towards his grandmother. Her home was always warm and welcoming with lots of framed photographs of her daughter Sara and grandson Dave almost completely covering one wall, and a photograph of her husband Jack on board HMS Unicorn taking pride of place; he died of rheumatic heart disease in 1952 just a few weeks before his daughter's second birthday.

The sound of a vehicle coming to a stop outside the bungalow pulled Dave from his reverie. Emblazoned on the side of the van was the name of the house clearance company, something which upset Dave deeply. 'This is the final goodbye Grandma' he whispered into the room, 'and then you're gone forever.'

Dave opened the door to two strangers who were about to remove many of his grandmother's earthly possessions from what was her home for more than fifty years.

'Don't take that chair!' Dave shouted as one of the men moved towards the red armchair. 'Start in the bedrooms and leave this room 'till last and don't take anything that hasn't got a yellow sticker on it, and take nothing from the bookshelf either'.

Palpitations grew stronger as Dave watched his grandmother's belongings being manhandled by strangers who carted them out to their van where they were being taken somewhere unknown and used by who knows who, or worst still destroyed. It took the men less than an hour to remove all yellow-stickered items and Dave watched their every move, the furrow on his forehead deepening as minutes ticked by until there was only a stillness occupying the room.

A light rain fell from a brighter sky following the downpour. Inside the bungalow tears flowed uncontrollably as Dave watched the van move off. He closed curtains to the outside world. The front room of the bungalow was now dark and empty of furniture except, that is, for the old red armchair which sat in the middle of the floor.

Dave managed to get his grandmother's chair into the back of his car once he'd manoeuvred various tools and boxes and laid down the back seats. It wasn't easy but he was determined it would fit into his little Peugeot 108. He sighed and patted the back of the chair murmuring, *'you're coming with me now Grandma.'*

Fortunately no one was home when Dave reached the house he shared with Jenna, but someone was watching him struggling to get the chair out of the car.

'What 'ave you got 'ere then Dave?'

'Hello Mr Jones, it's my late Grandma's chair and it means a lot to me' Dave said as he gently patted the chair back. 'I couldn't let it go to wherever house clearance pieces go could I?'

'At least you've got something to remember her by lad, although I reckon it needs recovering.'

'Oh no, I couldn't get it recovered, that'd take away all those memories.'

'Aye I suppose your right lad. Ere let me give you a hand.'

Mr Jones took the chair's cushion from the car, and Dave successfully manoeuvred the chair body carefully to the pavement.

Before handing over the cushion Mr Jones took a step back and pointed to the chair's seat.

'Look! There, where the cushion goes, there's something stuck in the groove at the back.'

'I'll take a look when I've got the chair indoors. By the way thanks for your help Mr Jones', Dave said cheerfully as the neighbour doffed his hat and continued on his way.

Earlier heavy rain left its mark on the sky with a rainbow and the prospect of a dry summer's evening, but the house was cold and it was only when Dave placed his grandmother's chair in the lounge that the room took on a warm atmosphere.

Dave took away the cushion and there *was* something stuck in the back groove of the seat; it looked like the corner point of a piece of white paper. He tried to retrieve it but the tiny piece his fingers gripped tore away as he pulled and there was nothing left to see. There was no time to waste as Jenna would soon be home and Dave wanted to get the chair into the spare bedroom before she had a chance to complain about an old chair ruining the look of her otherwise pristine lounge.

In Dave's opinion Jenna was a perfectionist in every sense of the word, from her personal appearance with her perfectly coiffured black hair and smart clothes, to every piece of expensive furniture having to be positioned in each room exactly where it must remain. He had previously suggested she might consider taking advice on her obsessiveness, but she insisted her attitude was not an obsession but simply her own imposed aesthetics. He decided not raise the subject again.

Their relationship had become strained over the past months and Dave racked his brain trying to work out why. He had been Executor to his grandmother's Will, a job he willingly took on, and the wide-ranging role caused him to compartmentalise the Jenna dilemma, but he knew whatever the underlying problem within their relationship he had to face it sooner or later.

'Dave I'm home, where are you? I'm late because I've been talking with Angie. You remember her don't you, and would you believe she has another man in her life? I'm worn out just imagining her life never mind living it. How d'you fancy going out for a meal this evening to celebrate?'

Dave reached the bottom of the stairs.

'Celebrate what?' he asked in amazement, and with some trepidation.

'Oh hi; there you are.'

'What are we celebrating?'

Jenna hung her raincoat on her own special hook on the wall by the front door, folding back its sleeves and straightening the collar. 'Celebrating you clearing Emma's bungalow at last; what else is there to celebrate?' she answered indignantly.

'What d'you mean at last?'

'Well she's been dead two months; don't you think it's time to sell the mausoleum and move on?'

'How can you say that? You know Emma's been both a grandmother and mother to me since I was a young child. Haven't you lost anyone you loved that much?'

'Can't say I have actually' Jenna quipped as she went bounding up the stairs.

Dave looked on in despair, shocked at his partner's coldness and lack of empathy, and remembered he hadn't closed the bedroom door.

A scream wafted down the stairs and through the floorboards.

'What the *fuck* is that thing doing in *my* bedroom?'

Dave took a beer from the fridge and waited for Jenna's ranting to stop.

Still screaming abuse she stormed downstairs. 'I'm not having that old, moth-eaten, smelly object in *my* house so you can take it to the tip and if you don't *I'll* throw both you and that eyesore out! You didn't even ask my permission!'

'Ask your permission? Why on earth would I need to do that; Emma was my grandmother.'

'Exactly, and this is *my* house in case you've conveniently forgotten!'

'I'm not likely to forget that, am I? Anyway I was thinking of moving into the bungalow now I've sorted out the transfer documents so I'll leave and save you the trouble of throwing me out.'

'Good idea, I'm *sick* of hearing about your amazing *Grandma* and how you're going to miss her, so move your stuff out first thing tomorrow, and as its Saturday you'll be able to get your mucky van-driving mate Pete to help.'

Dave stomped up the stairs to the spare bedroom and flopped into the chair. Holding his head in his hands he whispered *'what a day Grandma!'* He took in a deep breath just as his mobile rang.

'Hi Pete, fantastic timing; I was just about to ring you. Any chance you can put me up for the night?'

'Blimey matey what's wrong? Has Jenna gone off on one again?'

'Yes, I've had enough now. You wouldn't believe how uncaring, insensitive and downright hateful she is.'

'Oh yes I would; how many times have I tried to warn you she's a selfish, arrogant, money grabbing bitch, and I should know I dated her for a couple of weeks years ago didn't I, and that was long enough. You thought she'd changed, but a leopard never loses its spots matey.'

'I've decided to move into Grandma's bungalow so I could do with your van to take my stuff over. Any chance you can give me a hand tomorrow?'

'Of course matey but what if I bring the van round now, then when we get to mine we'll have a few beers to celebrate you coming to your senses.'

Dave breathed a sigh of relief.

'Phew! That would be great; thanks. I'll get my suitcases packed, and if you could bring over a couple of empty boxes for the rest of my stuff that would help; I've nothing large to take apart from Grandma's chair.'

'You've kept your grandmother's chair, the red one?'

'Yes, that's what sparked tonight's row; Jenna's livid and wants it gone so I'm leaving with it.'

Pete could hardly control his pleasure at Dave's news and said he was glad they could get back to pre-Jenna days when they regularly went to Abbey Stadium to watch Cambridge United play at home. 'Give me half an hour to organise things here' he told him, 'and I'll get to you around seven. See you then.'

The atmosphere in Jenna's house was toxic.

'So, your used car salesman mate's coming over for you?' Jenna yelled up the stairs. 'You'd better make sure that bloody chair goes with you or it'll be cinders by the time you get back.'

'You know he's got his own successful business but trust you to be derogatory, and anyway what makes you think I'm coming back?'

'Pete'll be able to bring his van round tomorrow won't he? How else will you get your stuff to Saint Emma's?'

Dave's patience was wearing thin as he stormed downstairs.

'I've already got my suitcases out ready to pack. It's not as if I've anything big to move, except for the chair of course, so I'll be no more than an hour and...' he snapped his fingers directly in front of Jenna's face, ...'I'll be out of your life forever, thank God! You've shown no understanding of how I feel about my grandmother's death, how I had to organise her funeral, sort out finances and arrange clearing out her home. You're an unsympathetic, egotistical bitch! Look around you! *This* place is a mausoleum; it's not *lived* in, not like Grandma's where there was warmth as soon as she opened the front door. You're a typical *ice queen*!'

'How dare you! If I'm an ice queen you're obviously not hot enough to melt me are you? You haven't minded living with me over the past three months, but suddenly it needs a worn out, misshapen, smelly old chair to make you happy? You're crazy!'

'Actually, *bitch*, I've hated living here and would've left months ago only for Grandma's illness and death.' Dave opened the drinks cabinet and took out four bottles of wine and, looking directly at Jenna, gave a chuckle, 'and if you think I'm leaving this quality stuff here you're mistaken; I bought these and they're coming with me.'

Still smiling, Dave left a stunned Jenna downstairs and went upstairs to finish packing.

Jenna refused to open the door to Pete so Dave did and greeted him by handing him one of his suitcases before following him to his van with the other, returning with two large empty cardboard boxes. Within just twenty minutes they had the chair in the van along with filled cardboard boxes. Pete started up the engine and drove off. Dave followed in his Purgeot.

'Where do you want this chair matey, by the fireplace?

'Perfect; thanks Pete.'

'It's a bit empty in here but it looks as though you've got enough to be going on with, and that was a good move of yours to keep your old bed. If you want company to get a few more bits and pieces I'm not working Monday.'

'Thanks I'd appreciate that and thank goodness for school holidays. Monday's fine, and if there's stuff I can pick up right away your van will be a Godsend.'

'Okay that's sorted. Next on the agenda is back to mine; Sandy's got grub ready so you can relax and have a few beers before you get a good night's sleep, which you deserve matey.'

Chapter Two

Moving On

August 2019

After a hearty breakfast with Pete and Sandy Dave drove to the home he could now officially call his own.

There was plenty of organising to do because Dave's suitcases and boxes were simply dropped in the hall the night before.

Throwing his belongings into suitcases and boxes was the easy part, but now Dave had to find hangers for his clothes and, luckily, he still had his old bed which his grandmother always kept made up ready for when her grandson stayed over. When Dave opened what was his old wardrobe he found it filled with empty wooden hangers, and each drawer he pulled open was lined with paper. He shook his head, smiled and whispered, '*Trust you Grandma; always ready for my return. I do love you!*'

With his clothes on hangers and in drawers and his few personal possessions placed back on shelves, Dave stood in the quiet of the front room and thought this was a good time to treat himself to a writing desk. He recalled Jenna complaining officiously when his students' homework was spread across her highly polished mahogany dining table and decided having a suitable desk would be comfortable to sit at and could be closed if anyone unexpected turned up. He searched local auction websites for both a writing desk and a dining table with four chairs, breathing a sigh of relief as he closed down his computer.

Emma always had plenty of food in her kitchen cupboards and, although Dave threw away some fresh food shortly after her death, there were packets and tins galore in what she laughingly called her very own M&S store cupboard. He busied himself by cleaning the fridge and small freezer in readiness for his food shopping spree. His weekend was so busy he had no time to ponder over his split with Jenna, and in no time at all the evening was drawing in. He ordered a pizza, got showered and dressed in his pj's and opened one of his favourite wines, a Cabalié; a richly spiced red with an illustrious medal winning history. He raised his glass, *'Cheers Grandma'* he said softly, *'Life is certainly looking better from here.'*

As promised Pete arrived at nine on Monday morning and was pleasantly surprised to find Dave ready and eager to go. They immediately set off to the auction room to buy the dining table and chairs and small writing desk Dave had chosen on line. Once that purchase was secured, Dave went on to M&S to buy bedding and order a dark red two-seater bed-settee which *almost* matched his grandmother's old chair.

Throughout the week Dave busied himself redecorating and getting used to living in what was now his own home, and was comfortable feeling his grandmother's love and warmth still enveloped him.

On Friday afternoon he was absorbed in tackling the small overgrown front garden when he heard someone call his name. At first he couldn't see who it was, only a blurred outline of a woman surrounded by sunlight. He was dazzled and skewed his eyes in the vain hope he would see her more clearly.

'Hello Dave. Don't you recognize me?' The vision enquired.

'Sorry. The sun's in my eyes; I can't see you that well.'

'It's Angela. I was sorry to hear your grandmother passed away. Are you still sorting things out or are you living here now?'

'Thanks. I've only just moved in.'

Dave got up from weeding the border and moved closer toward the vision that was Angela and gasped; he'd forgotten just how naturally beautiful she was. She'd grown tall and her long, golden-blonde hair glistened in the sunlight. Dave was dumbstruck.

As children Angela and Dave attended the same local schools although Angela, being two years younger, didn't see much of him. They met up at college but as happens with many student friendships the passage of time caused them to lose touch with each other. Their conversation was mainly around Emma, her illness and death, although they did talk a little about life in general and how each of them came to be living close to each other once again.

Dave noticed Angela didn't mention Jenna or that they'd met up recently, and this prompted him to bring Jenna into the conversation.

'Didn't Jenna tell you I'd moved out then? I thought you two were friends.'

'I haven't seen Jenna for months; we were only acquaintances through a mutual friend.'

Feeling somewhat confused Dave apologised for making such an assumption.

'So,' he said, 'have you got a new man in your life?'

'A new man, you must be joking! I was married but divorced Chris a year ago when I found he'd been having an affair with his secretary. I'm back at home with Mum now and I certainly haven't regretted *not* having a man in my life; I think I've been put off men forever anyway!'

Angela looked at her watch.

'I think it's time I let you get on with your gardening Dave; I've really enjoyed our chat. Bye for now.'

Dave looked on as Angela walked away from 2 Rosemary Close. He was angry, not only for talking about Jenna but especially for not suggesting to Angela they meet up for a drink. A wasp buzzed around his head causing him to eventually close his jaw.

As late afternoon brought a darkening sky with the prospect of another storm, Dave cleared away the gardening tools and went indoors. Looking in the bathroom mirror he was surprised to see his reflection was smiling back at him. His inner self admitted Angela definitely made an impression on him. He laughed out loud and winked to his mirror image before saying, *'Well, you never know maybe she'll pass by again.'*

By morning the storm had passed and Saturday brought with it a clear sky and the promise of sunshine.

Washing his breakfast dishes and staring out the kitchen window Dave revisited the sudden outburst of verbal abuse from Jenna which erupted simply because he'd deposited his grandmother's chair in her spare bedroom. She expected the bungalow to be totally cleared of furniture in order for it to be put on the open market for sale which Dave had previously told her was not going to be the case, and so was immediately reduced to blatant disgust at the sight of the catalyst, the old red chair. Dave shook his head in bewilderment wondering why so soon after his grandmother's death Jenna had been keen for the bungalow to be sold, which would have left Dave homeless once he moved out of the home he shared with Jenna.

'*Not that I'm bothered*' he said out loud as he rinsed the sink of soapsuds.

He sighed, dried his hands and gripped the edge of the Butler's sink as he once again stared through the window. He recounted the events of his life since his grandmother's death and the lack of understanding from Jenna for his grief, as well as her anger at his reluctance to sell the bungalow immediately. He reminded himself of when Jenna suggested he move in with her, insisting the mortgage remain in her sole name as, she said, she valued her financial independence and definitely didn't want that jeopardised. Dave's contribution was monetary in that he handed over sufficient money each month to cover the mortgage. This financial arrangement worked well but the sexual side of their relationship was on the wane for some time. He blamed himself and thought grief was the culprit, but now that he was seeing things more clearly he was aware there had been a lack of a friendly relationship, let alone a loving one, long before his grandmother's death in June. Sight of the red chair was enough to allow Jenna to break the few tenuous threads of their relationship. Although initially shocked, Dave was now content to feel genuine relief. He slapped his hands against the edge of the cool, white ceramic Butler's sink and exclaimed *'thanks Grandma, your chair proved to be the instrument of my salvation; you're definitely my guardian angel!'* His mobile phone vibrated across the worktop.

'Hi Pete, how are you?'

'Thankful it's the weekend if I'm honest matey; I've had a bloody awful few days at work.'

'Oh no, I'm sorry; what happened?'

'Two of the fitters got into a fight on the shop floor the other day and one ended up in hospital with a broken jaw!'

'Oh my God, your workers are normally a friendly lot; what caused the fight?'

'You remember Geoff, one of my best fitters, the short, tubby guy with receding hair. Well, he said he thought he was coming down with a virus so I told him to go home; that was just before lunch but he came back within half an hour, went straight over to Kev who'd just come on shift and laid into him! Apparently when Geoff was turning into his cul-de-sac Kev was driving past but didn't see him and when Geoff opened his front door his wife was standing there with a shocked expression and wearing only her bra and panties! Geoff made out he knew she'd been having an affair and was looking to catch her out and, would you believe it, she admitted she and Kev regularly got together when Geoff was at work, so poor old Geoff raced back here and belted the living daylights out of Kev! I disciplined both of them of course, and had one of the young lads take Kev to hospital. Geoff's taken a few days sick leave and although Kev came back yesterday he's been sent to Coventry by the rest of the men so the atmosphere's been tense. I just hope it eases off next week or I might have to consider laying Kev off for the sake of the business. We'll see.'

'So d'you want something energetic to do this weekend to take your mind off work; footie maybe?'

'Thanks matey that's not why I'm phoning, but maybe next weekend. No, Sandy and I thought we might go to that new Indian Ocean restaurant. D'you fancy coming with us?'

'I'd feel conscious being the extra to a couple but if I had someone to take I'd be up for it.'

'Bugger, I didn't think, sorry matey. If you change your mind we've booked for seven thirty.'

'Okay, thanks Pete. If I'm not there on the dot, start without me. Bye for now.'

Dave was in a quandary. He knew his grandmother kept an address book for people she wanted to send Christmas cards to, but couldn't remember seeing it when he'd searched drawers for her personal documents following her death. He was sure she would have had Angela's mother's address as she and Mrs Thomas were friends for years.

No address for Angela meant there was no chance he could ask her to join him for dinner so he drove into town to buy food for the weekend. He was in a daydream as he placed his groceries in bags and didn't hear a lady at the checkout behind calling him. It was only when the cashier interrupted his dreaming to have him pay that he heard his name called.

'Dave Wilson! So nice to hear you've moved into Emma's bungalow; I remember you were very happy there.'

At first he didn't recognise her, but when she said Angela was pleased to have met up with him again he was elated and saw this as his chance to contact her daughter. Their conversation continued outside the store as Dave walked Abigail Thomas to her car hoping to coax an address from her.

Back home and sitting in his grandmother's red chair Dave wrote a note to Angela. He felt a surge of excitement at the prospect of spending the evening with the once junior school run of the mill student who evolved into a beautiful woman. He walked to 16 Lavender Close and, avoiding being seen, gently pushed his note through the letterbox. The note included his mobile number and he asked Angela to call as there was something he wanted to ask her.

Later that afternoon there was a knock at Dave's front door. He was taken aback at seeing Angela standing on the step, her hands in her jacket pockets and wearing a frown rather than the smile he'd seen yesterday.

'Your note was a bit vague.'

With a heavy heart Dave invited her in, so sure she would turn his dinner invitation down. As soon as she entered the lounge Angela pointed to a chair she recognised.

'You've still got your grandmother's red chair!' she exclaimed, 'I'm so glad you kept it; can I sit in it?'

'Of course you can. I'll make some tea and I've even got biscuits!'

'Thanks Dave, I'd love a cup of tea; milk no sugar.'

A sense of relief wafted over Dave, but when he returned with a tray of tea and biscuits he was shocked to see Angela wiping tears from her eyes. He put the tray on the coffee table.

'What on earth's wrong Angela?'

'I don't know why I'm so upset' she said with a half smile but a croaky voice. 'Mum and Emma were good friends for years and I just got an image of being here with Mum when the Police turned up with you in your pyjamas. Emma took you from the officer and sat down with you in this chair and wept. I was only two going on three and didn't understand what was going on, but when I was older Mum told me your mum and dad had been killed in a road accident. She said the woman looking after you that night told the Police that when your mum opened the door her face was bruised and she'd been crying. She told the police the way your mum was acting she thought your dad had forced her to go out with him that night. Sitting in this chair I can feel your grandmother's distress. I'm sorry Dave I didn't think I'd get so upset after all these years.'

Dave felt a rush of emotion and immediately knelt in front of Angela, holding both her hands in his.

'Don't be sorry' he said softly. 'That must've been scary for a two-year-old to see and hear, and the emotion has obviously stayed with you. Somehow I put all that out of my mind and must have refused to revisit it, but obviously being spoiled by Grandma helped. These days there's lots of counselling organisations but there was nothing like that when I was a kid, you just had to accept the bad things and get on with life.'

'Oh gosh, I'm so sorry Dave; I didn't mean to bring such unhappy memories back for you.'

'Grandma never spoke about the crash and I didn't question her. I don't know if she heard me but I cried myself to sleep for weeks. Gradually life felt sort of normal, and luckily for me everything turned out okay.'

Dave handed Angela a mug of tea. She stayed sitting in the chair and Dave stood, one arm leaning across the stone fire grate mantel and they chatted about their lives since high school. Angela said she moved to London having obtained a place at the London College of Fashion, later opening her own atelier in the artisan area of All Saints Road London. She went on to say that more recently she sold her fashion business and that's when she returned to live with her mother at Lavender Close. She was brimming with excitement as she told Dave she was about to complete her purchase of a workshop in nearby Cambridge city centre. Dave saw this as an opportunity for him to offer to help Angela set up her new workshop. He was keen to explain it wouldn't take long for him to get there from work and he would be happy to help at weekends.

Angela was delighted. 'Thank you so much Dave that would be great; there's so much to do' she said, beaming.

Dave told Angela about the fun he'd had on the last day of term when students were given the opportunity to throw wet sponges at teachers who stupidly placed themselves into wooden stocks, and how there seemed to be more soggy sponges being hurled at him than any other teacher.

When they stopped laughing Dave described the day of the house clearance and why he decided to keep the red velvet chair, and that prompted him to suddenly point to it.

'I've just remembered there's something sticking out from the frame. Do you think, with your small fingers and lovely long nails you might be able to pull out whatever's stuck in there?'

'Sounds intriguing but I don't want to damage my nails' Angela giggled as she got up from the chair. 'It's a good job I keep my eyebrow tweezers in my handbag, I'm sure they'll grip whatever's in the seat.'

Dave took away the cushion and knelt in front of the chair but try as he might he couldn't ease the back section of material from the base, and with Dave in that position Angela couldn't get close enough to the seat back to grab whatever was stuck inside. She suggested they lay the back of the chair on the floor as in that position Dave would be able to stand behind the base, bend over, put his fingers into the groove, get a grip on the material and pull it up.

'Trust a woman to come up with a logical idea' Dave said with a smile as he got up from his kneeling position and stood behind what was now the base of the chair. He leaned over ready to ease the base material up and away as Angela, now prone on the floor and pressing down on the back of the chair with tweezers at the ready, instructed him to grab hold and *pull*!

'Eureka! I can see something in there Dave; you pull up again and I'll push down this side and hopefully I'll get a grip.'

With that they started tittering and when Angela looked up towards Dave's face they both totally lost control, let go of the chair and rolled about the floor laughing. Eventually they composed themselves, but they were still giggling when they took up their positions again.

'I've got it!' Angela exclaimed as she teased out a creased piece of writing paper from its dark fissure and handed it up to Dave.

With the chair now in its natural position and cushion replaced, Dave sat on the settee alongside Angela but stared straight ahead, the note still crumpled in his hands.

'Aren't you going to read it?' Angela gently asked.

'I know it's stupid, but because it's obviously something Grandma wrote it's like she's still here and I feel a bit uneasy. Will you look at it?'

Angela took the note from Dave and eased out the creases with the palm of her hand to reveal the words... *Look in the attic for an engraved wooden box, my ditty box, and you'll understand why there are no photos of your father and what I think happened to*

Angela looked up at Dave. 'Emma must have been interrupted. She obviously intended to write more.'

'Let me see.'

Dave silently read the note while Angela looked on, her hand now resting gently on his knee.

'Are you okay Dave?'

'Yes, but I've just realised I could easily have sold the bungalow with Grandma's personal possessions left in the attic! I totally forgot to check; I feel awful. I wonder how much is up there.'

'I don't mind staying a bit longer if you want to look now.'

'I'm tempted, but have you seen the time? We've been talking for ages, and the reason I wanted you to phone me was so I could ask you to join me for dinner at the new Indian restaurant in town. Pete and Sandy invited me and I said if I wasn't there on the dot of seven thirty they should start without me.'

'That's a lovely idea Dave, thank you. I'd better get home and tell mum before she starts cooking tonight's meal with me in mind.'

Dave opened the front door.

'Now I know your address I'll pick you up. I'll be outside your house at a quarter past seven.'

He watched Angela's every move as she walked to the gate, opened and closed it behind her, smiled and waved and then disappeared from sight.

The restaurant was buzzing with atmosphere and chatter. Dave put his hand in the small of Angela's back as he escorted her to the table where Pete and Sandy were sitting.

As he pulled away a chair for Angela, Dave winked to Pete, 'so you went ahead and ordered a table for four; that was very forward thinking for you Pete.'

Pete stood and planted a couple of gentle kisses on Angela's cheeks. 'Glad to see you again Angela' he said, 'and twice in one day! But what's a beautiful woman like you doing with this reprobate, surely you know someone with more joie de vivre?'

'What was that?'

Pete laughed, 'Sorry Dave, maybe rogue is more appropriate!'

'No, you said twice in one day?'

Angela turned to Dave and he could see a feint flush beginning to cover her cheeks.

'I bumped into Pete and Sandy on my way home from yours and they said they'd asked you to join them for a meal but you probably wouldn't because you didn't have anyone to make up a foursome, so I told them you'd already invited me.'

Pete laughed so hard he almost choked on his beer.

Angela looked worried so Dave took hold of her hand and gently kissed it, before placing both his hands firmly on the table top and celebrated the benefits of having such amazing and interfering friends.

Pete raised his glass, 'Cheers matey!'

The evening was filled with friendly football banter between Pete and Dave, while Sandy and Angela compared some of their teenage escapades and the boys they fancied but have since seen and been glad they didn't end up with. The two women laughed so hard tears flowed.

'You remember Billy Shaw don't you Angela?' Sandy asked. 'He said I reminded him of the Mona Lisa with my long black hair, and he kept pestering me to go out with him but, imagine if I'd married *him*?'

'Why? He was quite good looking if I remember rightly.'

'I'd have been another Sandy Shaw and I can't even sing!'

'And you might have ended up a puppet on a string!'

The atmosphere at the table was jovial and both Dave and Angela were obviously glad they'd accepted the dinner invitation from Pete.

Being a newly opened restaurant the manager offered everyone a digestif on the house. Dave and Pete accepted a Brandy whilst Angela and Sandy chose the sweet Italian liqueur Amaretto.

'Service is great here isn't it matey? Maybe we should make this a regular night out.'

'I'm all for that Pete' Dave whispered as his eyes gestured toward Angela.

Conversation moved on to Dave moving back into his grandmother's home permanently, and Pete said he was surprised Dave kept his grandmother's old chair.

Before Dave could comment, Angela said excitedly 'The chair holds so many memories for Dave and between us we got that piece of paper from under the frame; you should have seen us Pete, we were both on the floor laughing at the positions we were in.'

'What piece of paper?' Pete exclaimed. 'That sounds mysterious, and *positions*; pray tell me your positions matey I might learn something' he laughed.

Obviously embarrassed, Angela apologised to Dave. 'That's okay' he said. 'It was Mr Jones, Jenna's neighbour, who saw the piece of paper sticking out of the chair back; Pete knows nothing about it.'

Pete's eyes widened as he sat back in his chair. 'C'mon then matey, what's the story?'

Dave told Pete and Sandy how the small corner of a piece of paper came to be found sticking out of the chair back and how he and Angela in various precarious positions managed to retrieve it. Once they'd all stopped laughing, Dave told them what his grandmother had written and said he'd go up to the attic tomorrow to find the wooden box.

The mood at the table became somewhat sombre and for a second or two no one spoke. Dave broke the silence by asking Angela if she'd come round to the bungalow about ten and help him find the box as he was sure he'd be asking her to read more of his Grandma's notes. She said she would. The evening came to a natural end, each couple thanking the other for a very pleasant and convivial evening.

Dave drove straight to Angela's home rather than invite her to his for a nightcap as he wasn't sure she'd accept. He brought the car to a stop.

'Thanks for agreeing to help me tomorrow.'

Angela looked down towards her cupped hands and Dave was tempted to lean across and kiss her, but although she lifted her head for the briefest of moments causing their eyes to meet, she simply whispered goodnight and gracefully stepped out of the car.

Watching Angela as she walked to her front door filled Dave with an emotion he'd never experienced before. He raised his hand to return her wave as she closed the door and the sense of loss he suddenly felt was overwhelming. He sat holding the steering wheel and staring ahead for a few minutes before moving off.

Chapter Three

Relationships

August 2019

'Good job the restaurant manager had my phone number matey!' Pete said as the front door opened to his broad grin early on Sunday morning. 'You left your mobile on the table and of course I couldn't phone to tell you could I? So here I am, and don't worry there's no delivery charge.'

'Blimey that's not like me is it?'

Pete laughed. 'No, but you were distracted by your beautiful companion weren't you?' He looked past Dave into the hallway and whispered, 'Blimey matey, she's not here is she?'

Dave chuckled. 'No, but was it that obvious last night?'

'She's grown into a good looking woman hasn't she?'

'Yes, and she's got a gentle and sympathetic manner too. Do you think I've got a chance with her?'

'That's up to you matey. She's a lady and a much better character than Jenna that's for sure.

I reckon all *she* was after was your money, and if you *had* sold your grandmother's bungalow I'll bet she would've been looking for a share of your inheritance. Oh, and by the way, rumour has it Kev was having it off with Jenna as well as Geoff's missus, so now Jenna's got Kev all to herself. Poor sod, he'll be sorry. So you see matey, you had a lucky escape. I reckon your grandmother's still looking after you.'

'Why have you brought a ladder? Is that your idea of a housewarming gift?'

'Not bloody likely! I need this ladder but I thought you'd need it today to get into the attic.'

'Good idea; why didn't I think of that?'

'Because matey, you're not thinking straight are you?'

'Grandma must've managed though, but I can't say I've ever seen a ladder here. I stood on an old table to do the decorating. Take it round to the back garden if you don't mind Pete and thanks again.'

Dave went through the house and met up with Pete in the garden.

'This needs a tidy up for sure matey' Pete remarked. 'Will you tackle it yourself or get someone in? Obviously Emma wasn't able to manage this when she became unwell. Such a shame; I really liked your grandmother.'

'I think I'll take my time with this. I've got a few ideas for a patio area and I can have friends round for a BBQ.'

'Well, provided of course I'm included in every BBQ I'll be more than happy to give you a hand with paving slabs etcetera. Just tell me when.'

'You're a good friend Pete. I won't forget this.'

'Don't worry matey, I won't let you' Pete laughed. 'And don't forget to keep me in the loop; I can't wait to find out what's in your Grandma's box. Bye for now.'

Chapter Four

Grandma's Box of Secrets

August/September 2019

'Have you found it yet?'

No answer.

'Have you found the box?'

No answer.

'Dave, are you okay?'

Angela was looking up to the hole in the ceiling as she leant against the ladder, one foot resting on the bottom rung. Dave had taken a large LED torch into the attic and every few minutes Angela saw his dark gigantic shadow move across the opening and disappear again.

'Dave I'm getting worried now. I told you I'm not good with heights so I'd rather not climb up to you; please come down.'

'You wouldn't believe what's up here.'

'Try me.'

'You'll have to come up and see for yourself.'

Angela gripped the sides of the ladder and laid her forehead against one cool rung. Her head was pounding at the thought of the distress she was about to suffer as she ascended the steps. 'I'm not sure I can do this' she said aloud, but eased her grip, looked up and started climbing.

'I knew you'd make it.'

With Dave's help Angela stepped into the attic seeing only darkness, but within a few seconds she saw him, his face lit by a low light.

Dave aimed the torchlight at one wall were there were photos and newspaper cuttings, stuck there haphazardly with sticky tape. For what seemed a very stretched few minutes both Dave and Angela stood in silence staring at the wall. Dave slowly moved the torchlight across each piece of paper and photograph. There were photos obviously taken at parties through the years when his mum and dad were teenagers, many showing groups of people smoking and drinking alcohol.

There were gaps in the years of photos, but there were images of his parents' 1977 wedding. His mum's wedding dress was white satin having long, flowing satin and lace sleeves with a wide, white ribbon under her bust leaving the straight skirt to tumble down to her white, flat shoes. Her long auburn hair, drawn back from her face in ringlets and falling over her shoulders, was covered with an abundance of tiny white daisies, and there was a small, silver daisy on a chain around her neck. Tiny fresh daisies were also attached to a beaded silver hair band, and these were echoed in her small bouquet. His dad wore a cream, large collared jacket covering an orange and yellow flower-patterned open necked shirt, and with his plain yellow flared trousers and shoulder length black hair he was still very much the hippy. He also wore a moustache which surprised Dave as he'd never pictured him with hair on his face.

Dave held the torchlight a little longer over the wedding picture.

'I don't remember ever seeing these photographs though,' Dave said in a hushed voice, 'and I didn't find a chain and daisy pendant in Grandma's jewellery box, so I wonder where they went.'

Angela looked closer at the necklace in the photograph, 'I think its silver; I doubt your mum would have got rid of it when it belonged to her daughter. Did you find *any* of your mum's jewellery?'

'There were a few pieces that looked like they'd belonged to Mum, just a few large daisy earrings and plastic bead necklaces and, when I come to think of it, her wedding ring wasn't in the jewellery box and surely Grandma would have kept that. It's strange seeing them so happy in these photos and yet they're not here anymore.'

'This style is flower power isn't it? I have to say I quite like it!' Angela said.

Dave suddenly morphed into teacher mode and answered in his classroom-like voice.

'The expression flower power was used to describe the peaceful movement of the time, rooted in the opposition against the Vietnam War which started in November 1955 to the fall of Saigon on 30th April 1975.'

'You definitely are a font of all knowledge Mr. Wilson' Angela teased.

Dave continued, 'I know that hippies of the sixties and seventies wore very colourful clothes and put flowers in their hair, and I read it was because once the country recovered from the effects of the war and post-war austerity young people needed to identify with their new-found freedom.'

'Ha! Then let's test your knowledge again *Sir*; what historical event happened the year your mum and dad married?'

'That's not fair! Hold on, I know; Steve Jobs and Steve Wozniak created Apple! *And*, if I'm not mistaken that was the year Concorde went into service. How's *that* Miss Thomas?'

Angela laughed, 'I don't know! All I know about computers relates to sorting out my accounts, and as for Concorde I just know it had a pointed nose and very expensive seats!'

'Did *your* mum ever talk to you about what she got up to when she was young?'

'She did say there was supposed to be a lot of free love and plenty of sex around in the 60's and 70's but she never found any' Angela giggled, '*not*, of course that she necessarily went looking for it she insists. God forbid! Her parents would have disowned her after her father had given her what they used to call a good hiding!'

The mood having been lightened a little, Dave continued to move the torchlight across the wall when he suddenly went into reverse and laid the light back onto the wedding photo.

Angela spoke first. 'You don't look like your dad do you? He's short with black hair, but there is such a thing as a throwback you know, where you could look like someone in the family alive years before you. Maybe there was a tall, blonde, handsome male ancestor in your family.'

Dave turned the torchlight directly on Angela's face. 'So you think I'm handsome do you?'

Angela screwed up her eyes and gently dug her right elbow into Dave's ribs.

'Get on with your search please Sherlock; now I'm here I'm interested to see what else your grandmother kept in her attic.'

Accepting Angela's explanation as to why he looked so unlike the man in the wedding photograph, Dave moved the torchlight across the wall, highlighting newspaper cuttings from various papers, then stopping at a headline which read *A 200 vehicle pileup on the M6 in thick fog was responsible for the death of ten people with over sixty injured.* He moved on, stopping momentarily at cuttings from local newspapers, coming across an image of a road he recognised and reference made to September fog. The reporter commented on skid marks curving from the road towards a verge beyond which a motorbike lay broken and almost wrapped around a tree trunk signifying, alleged the reporter, high speed and a lack of control by the driver as yet unnamed.

Dave looked around for Angela. He saw her mobile phone torch lighting up the attic space around her as she walked towards him.

'I found the box' Angela said softly, 'it was on top of that small metal trunk over there'. She directed her light to the trunk which Dave could now see was sitting very close to the opening into the attic. 'I moved back here as I got a bit dizzy and was frightened I'd fall.'

Dave put his arms around Angela and hugged her.

'I'm sorry. I didn't realise you'd be affected so badly.'

'I'm okay now I've moved over here.'

'This is like a Police incident room. Grandma must have come up here and done all this after Mum died, but why, unless she didn't want me to know what she was trying to work out.'

With the bright light from Dave's torch the images became eerily visible.

'There are some photos of you here Dave!'

Dave didn't speak.

'Who are you with here, a girlfriend? She's beautiful. Someone's written something at the bottom but the ink's a bit faded.' Angela shone her light on the writing and moved closer. 'I've got it! It says "outside Moderna Museet Stockholm".' Angela looked across to Dave who was staring at her.

'I've never been to Stockholm' Dave whispered.

The cool air within the attic began to envelope Angela and caused her to shiver violently. 'Let's take all this down with us Dave' she said. 'There's no point in trying to see everything just by the light of a torch.'

Without speaking, but responding to Angela's suggestion, Dave began to peel away the newspaper cuttings and photographs from the attic wall and descended the ladder, his left arm held tightly against his chest to clutch the information he and Angela had found. Having deposited everything on the coffee table in the front room he returned and reached out to Angela to retrieve the box from her before guiding her safely down the ladder in silence.

Faded newspaper cuttings and photos lay across the coffee table, with the ornate wooden box set to one side. Dave and Angela looked on; mesmerised.

Dave broke the silence. 'I'll go back up later to check what's in the trunk. Would you mind staying for a while and I'll pass down whatever's inside? If there's too much in there I'll get Pete to give me a hand to bring the whole thing down.'

'Of course I will.'

The box is best described as being an oblong, narrow casket made of intricately carved Indian sandalwood with a keyhole but no key. Dave opened the lid to find a neat row of bundles of envelopes, each bundle tied with yellow ribbon.

'Look at all these letters! Where do I start?'

Dave picked one bundle from the left, assuming his Grandma's natural idea of tidiness was to start there with the earliest letters. His hands were shaking as he opened the first letter dated Tuesday 25 March 1969 which he read to himself ...*How I miss you my darling Sara x If only you could be here we would be celebrating my birthday staying in bed and making love through Sunday like John Lennon and Yoko Ono xx I'm imagining stroking your beautiful silky smooth skin....*

Dave put the letter back in its envelope. 'I can't read these' he said, 'this one's from someone named Lars and he's talking about staying in bed and making love! They're all probably intimate love letters, and he's writing to my *mother*! Well, years before I was born obviously, but why did Mum keep them, and how did Grandma end up with them?'

'More to the point, is it Sara in this picture? If it *is* her, the man might be Lars.'

'This is weird; it certainly looks like her.'

Angela picked out an envelope from the other end of the casket. 'If the letters are sequential, check the date on this one as it might be the last.'

'Oh my God, this one's addressed to Grandma and has the date 30 September 1982 signed Lars Anderson.'

Angela leaned forward. 'You'll have to read it; do you mind if I look on?'

Apart from the gentle ticking of the pendulum wall clock there was no sound in the room as Dave's and Angela's eyes moved across the words Lars had written.

Dear Mrs Thomas

We have never met and I'm sorry if writing this will upset you but my Sara said to tell you the truth if anything happened to her. Sara knew I kept all her letters and said I should send those to you too.

Many times my Sara travelled to England for her work and when she was there she lived with you. Sara's newspaper editor sent her to London to report on King Olaf of Norway attending the funeral of his cousin the Duke of Windsor on 5 June 1972. You will remember she was expecting our child. We have a daughter her name is Ann and she is beautiful just like her mamma. Ann was born on 26 December 1972. We were very happy.

You know that Sara returned to her work as a journalist in Amsterdam and often travelled to England where her newspaper opened an office in

London, and when she was there she lived with you, but she was with us for Christmas and Ann's birthday in 1976 before returning to England in January 1977. Sara came back to Bergen for my birthday in March and we were blissfully happy for the few days she spent here. I thought my Sara was so happy she would stay but before she left she told me she was going to marry Barry Wilson who she had known since schooldays, and so we thought we'd lost her forever. Ann was deeply upset. That was very sad, but in May 1977 Sara came to Netherlands to report news for her English paper of a train hijacking, killing and children hostages. The story upset her so much she became unwell and lived here for a week with her family.

I am sending you a letter Sara wrote to me on Sunday 20 June 1982 and you can see she was unhappy with her marriage and was coming back to live with us forever. Ann was excited and we both wanted to see Sara very much.

Your granddaughter is twelve this year and when we heard of my Sara's death we were distressed. Maybe you will write to Ann at my address and maybe you will allow us to visit you in England. You will love your granddaughter and she is made in Sara's image.

Lars and Ann x

The clock seemed to be ticking louder. Angela put her arm around Dave's shoulder as he turned his head to face her. They hugged each other. The clock was chiming one o'clock as they released their hold. Dave was the first to speak.

'I have a half-sister! Why didn't anyone tell me?'

'Maybe your grandmother was simply trying to shield you from the truth as it would hurt you to know your mum left her daughter in Amsterdam all those years ago to come back here and marry your father. Anyway, as the child was eleven when your mum died in eighty-two she'd be of an age when she might say she didn't want to meet her English family, and if your grandmother got in touch with her and she rebuffed her she would have been devastated. It could be she thought things were best left as they were but, bless her, she kept all these letters so did want you to know at some point that you had a sister. Ann will be in her forties now and probably married with her own children; she obviously didn't contact her grandmother, and Lars hasn't written since that letter.'

Angela took the now scrunched up letter from Dave's hands, straightened and folded it before placing it back in its envelope. 'He mentions enclosing Sara's letter but it's not here. What are you going to do, write to him?'

Dave buried his face in his hands before running them through his hair, a frown simultaneously erupting on his forehead. He stared ahead and stood up, pulling back his shoulders allowing his arms to fall by his sides. Angela put her hand out to touch his but he moved forward leaving her outstretched arm hanging in the air.

He walked over to the red chair and sat down, caressed its arms and then brought his hands down with force, shouting 'Why the *hell* didn't you tell me Grandma?'

Angela knelt in front of Dave and put her hands over his. When he lifted his head tears were welling in his eyes. 'There's so much I don't know!' he cried.

'I'm certain your grandmother did what she did, or didn't do anything as it seems, to save you from being upset, so try to understand her reasoning; she loved you dearly and wouldn't deliberately want to hurt you.'

Dave rubbed his hands across his eyes and cheeks, 'Phew! Sorry about that' he said.

Angela got up and walked over to the settee. 'I think some fresh air will help' she said, 'it's one-thirty and I don't know about you but all this detective work's made me hungry. Mum will be cooking dinner so let's go and enjoy a Sunday roast. I'll call her and ask her to set one more place at the table; she'll be happy to see you I promise.'

Dave's previous idea of a walk with Angela was quite different to the one she was talking about now, but a walk is a walk he thought. He waved his hands across the once-hidden story of his mother's life, declaring 'I'm not in the right frame of mind to go through any more of this stuff, or go back up to the attic anyway. I'll freshen up and yes, that sounds like a great idea; thanks.'

Chapter Five

Is there anybody there?

August/September 2019

It was almost midnight when Dave returned home.

When saying goodnight to Dave, Angela told him the furnishings for her new workshop were not being delivered until Wednesday which, she insisted, gave her a few days free to help him get to grips with his grandmother's revelations.

Good company and a succulent Sunday roast dinner cooked to perfection in the old fashioned way was something Dave hadn't experienced since his last lunch with his grandmother some three months before her death, and it was a welcome distraction from thinking about the many photos, notes and letters strewn across his coffee table and floor. He was determined not to get involved in looking through them again until Monday. He switched the hall light on and walked straight ahead with the intention of going to his bedroom when something caught his attention. He turned back.

Dave stood stock-still in the doorway of what his grandmother always called her front room; he scratched his head and looked around. The furrows on his forehead deepened. *'I'm sure I didn't move the chair'* he whispered into the now cool air. He pointed to the chair, *'and I definitely saw Angela put the box on the table not the chair!'* There being no earthly explanation for these changes, Dave closed the door on the mystery and headed for his bed.

Dave woke at seven. He drew back the bedroom curtains to a beautifully sunny Monday morning.

Looking out the window with his hands lying softly on the wooden sill Dave smiled then slapped the sill, turned around and started punching the air above him as he walked to the door of his bedroom. *'Well!'* Dave exclaimed to the room *'I reckon this is going to be another good day!'*

He danced into the hall singing *'I think I love you so what am I so afraid of, I'm afraid I'm not sure of, a love there is no cure for...'*

Still in his pj's Dave skipped up the hall towards the front room. He stopped, suddenly remembering that the chair and box had been moved but not by him. He gingerly opened the door and looked around the frame before stealthily walking in and opening the curtains. The chair and box were as they were the night before. Dave ran his fingers through his hair. *'What are you up to Grandma?'* he said aloud to the chair before slowly removing the box and placing it back on the coffee table. He left the chair where it was.

The temptation to sift through his grandmother's notes and the box was strong, but Dave managed to control the urge and went into the kitchen to set up his breakfast. He'd bought bacon, sausage, eggs and black pudding but decided against cooking a full fry-up as he didn't want the bungalow to smell like a trucker's cafe when Angela came over. They'd agreed eight o'clock as both of them were early risers. Cornflakes, toast and coffee was the only other option available.

Dave opened the patio door of the dining kitchen and sat eating his breakfast whilst trying to work out the conundrum which was the moving of the chair and box. Still holding his coffee mug and in a state of mind transcending any earthly thoughts, he imagined his grandmother turning up last night and choosing to move the chair from beside the fireplace to a position closer to the coffee table, and then taking the box off the coffee table and placing it on the chair. He was still in this trance state when the doorbell rang. It was rung for a second time.

'Hold on a minute!'

When he opened the front door Angela was standing there open mouthed. 'You're in your pyjamas!' she laughed.

'Oh! Sorry, what time is it?'

'It's five to eight!'

'Come in and, again, I'm sorry. I've been up for ages but got lost in my thoughts. Wait 'till you hear what I found last night!'

'Oh that sounds exciting!'

'I wouldn't say that, but it was certainly a surprise. I'll clear away my breakfast and make us some coffee.'

'No, you get dressed and I'll make coffee; just point me in the right direction for coffee and cups and I'll be fine.'

Dressed in jeans and a short sleeved loose, grey T-shirt emblazoned with the words *Of course I talk to myself - Sometimes I need expert advice*! Dave bounded back into the kitchen just in time to relieve Angela of two mugs of coffee and follow her into the front room.

'Do you remember where Grandma's chair was yesterday?' Dave asked with a friendly smile.

Angela pointed towards the fireplace. 'It was over there.'

'Exactly, but where is it now?'

Angela couldn't speak; she just looked wide-eyed at Dave who picked up the wooden box and placed it on the seat of the chair. 'And that's where the box was last night.'

'Did your grandmother move them?'

'Who else would do that, but I wish I knew why?'

'Might she be trying to tell you to sit in the chair and look through the letters in the box right away?'

'That's what I was thinking so I guess that's where we start then. Are you going to sit in the chair or should I?'

'You must sit in it Dave. Not that I'm frightened, your grandmother wouldn't harm a fly, but as her grandson your connection to her is stronger than mine and if there's any spiritual influence at work here you're the one to pick it up.'

'Okay, let's get started on the letters.'

Time ticked by. Dave and Angela didn't speak as they opened up letter after letter until Angela came across a letter from Sara to Lars dated Sunday 20th June 1982.

'Here's Sara's letter Lars refers to in his' Angela said as she unfolded it to read aloud.

My dearest Lars

I can't live this lie any more so I'm going to leave Barry. My time with you and Ann this year made me realise how much I love you both and I miss you so much.

Barry's been an absolute arsehole! Sorry for the bad language but it's what he is. He's not the man I thought he was when I married him – I know I've told you that already haven't I? He's been drinking more than ever and all he wants to do when he gets back from the pub is hurt me in every sense of the word. He gets angry very easily and hits out at me too, but thankfully he's never touched Dave. I'm bruised in places you wouldn't believe!

As soon as I can sort things out here and book a flight I'll let you know. Dave's too young for me to tell him what's happening and if I make out we're going on a holiday he'll probably tell Barry and all hell will break loose. I don't want to tell mum until I've got things sorted, but if something happens to me please keep in touch with her. Bless her, every time a letter arrives from you at her house she puts it in her beautiful wooden ditty box in her wardrobe so that when we visit her Barry's never likely to see them. It's a Godsend she's ready to help me sort things out. I don't know how I'd cope without her.

Keep well my darling and I'll write again soon.

Sx

Angela handed the letter to Dave, his eyes wide open. 'She was going to leave me with *dad*?' he said weakly.

'I doubt that very much Dave especially as she says if you think you're going on a holiday you might say something to Barry. She was obviously in a bad place and trying to put her life in order, which of course included you.'

'So, let me try to get this straight in my head. Mum and my dad knew each other as teenagers. Mum and Lars met when she was a journalist in Amsterdam, but mum didn't marry Lars although they lived together and had a child in 1971. Mum's newspaper opened an office in England and posted her there and that's where she met up again with my dad; they got married in 77. She left Ann with Lars? I can't get my head around that Angela.'

'Who knows what the circumstances were for your mum at that time. She and Lars might have been ready to break up, or maybe she didn't want Danish citizenship and her escape was when her newspaper opened the office in England. Your mum wouldn't have left Ann unless Lars was able to give her a good home and education, and of course Amsterdam was, and is Ann's home. I wonder if he got married after your mum died.'

'He might be dead now!'

'Surely he'd only be about seventy, and that's not old these days.'

'Just think if he's still alive he could have lived a habit of fathering children outside marriage and there could be lots more Lars Anderson's around now.'

'Don't be so insensitive Dave!'

'Sorry, that was uncalled for; I've obviously spent too much time in Jenna's company, but honestly, I'm a bit shaken by all this information and why Grandma hid it rather than talk to me about it when I was older.'

'There doesn't seem to be anything here to say your grandmother did get in touch with Lars or Ann; that's a shame. It's 2019 and Ann was born in 1972 so she'll be forty-seven. You could try to reach her.'

'I'm not sure I want to. She might be married with a family of her own now so why mess that up. Let's get back to working out this tangled web because I've just had a thought! Mum and dad married in spring 1977 didn't they? And I was born November 77. Do you see where I'm going with this?'

'But you don't know for sure when she left Amsterdam.'

'We'll have to find out. She might have married dad because she was pregnant with me, and what if my father wasn't Barry but Lars? I wonder how mum felt when I popped out with a mop of blonde hair.'

Dave laughed awkwardly.

'*Next*' he said sadly 'the million dollar question is did dad, Barry Wilson, deliberately drive his bike into the tree intending to kill Mum because she was going to leave him and take me with her?'

Angela and Dave stared at each other. The clock ticked on loudly, filling the room with its rhythmic sound. The now cool and tense atmosphere prevailed for what felt like minutes rather than seconds.

The sound of something falling to the floor caused Angela to physically jump up.

'What was that?' she shouted.

Dave stood and put his arms around Angela's shoulders. 'Don't be frightened, I think its Grandma.'

Angela pulled away from Dave. She stared directly at him. 'How can that be, and more to the point, even if she could drop something on the floor, why would she?'

Dave took hold of Angela's hands. She was still shaking and her hands were cool to the touch. He gently pulled her towards him and she didn't resist. They held on to each other, two bodies standing as one in the centre of the room. The nervous atmosphere gradually eased into one of warmth and love as Angela and Dave slowly uncoupled. Their eyes met. Dave cupped Angela's face and tenderly kissed her lips which immediately parted to accept him.

Angela gently broke away, 'What if your grandmother can see us?' she whispered.

Dave roared with laughter. 'You silly sausage, if she could she'd be happy.'

'*Silly sausage*' Angela exclaimed. 'What flavour am I then?'

'Come back here and I'll check'.

Tentatively, Angela moved back into Dave's arms. His kiss was gentle, passionate and thrilling and his excitement was obvious.

'Well, what do you think?' Angela asked.

'Think about what, the kiss?'

Angela coyly thumped Dave's shoulder. 'No. The type of sausage of course!

'Oh, I can't be sure. I'll have to rethink that one so let me check again.'

Once again Dave's kiss aroused Angela, and when she leaned away Dave whispered, 'Bratwurst, yes definitely Bratwurst.'

'*Bratwurst!*'

'Yes; it's a delicious and fragrant sausage, well seasoned and spiced.'

'So I smell okay, I'm old but hot?'

'And you taste delicious.'

'Is this going where I think it might be going?'

'I certainly hope so.'

'What about your grandmother?'

Dave's laugh was loud and contagious causing Angela to shed tears of happiness. When their laughter subsided, Angela suggested maybe they should first check what had fallen and come back to follow up the kiss later.

'You must be joking' whispered Dave as he led her away from the front room.

Chapter Six

Grandma's Precious Books

August/September 2019

Two happy and satisfied lovers, one dressed only in shorts sitting in a chair whilst silently picking through papers lying on a table, the other wearing only a shirt and walking barefoot into the room conveyed a truly comfortable scene. The couple smiled lovingly at each other as Angela handed Dave a mug of steaming coffee.

Angela sat on the edge of the settee. 'I can't believe we fell asleep after, after making love' she stuttered. 'Have you seen the time?'

Dave sat back in the chair and draped one leg casually over the other. 'I haven't felt this good in years and I actually don't care *what* time it is.'

Angela smiled and lowered her head. 'I know exactly how you feel; I feel the same.' Raising her head she looked straight into Dave's dark blue eyes. 'Isn't it strange how we came to meet up again? I think your grandmother had a hand in this, don't you?'

'Definitely, and the more I think about it the more obvious her intervention becomes. It's just a pity she didn't try to get us together while she was alive, she would've been so proud of herself.'

Angela chuckled 'Just like Jane Austen's character her namesake Emma, she decided to become a matchmaker, but this time from the other side.'

Dave put down his cup, got up from his chair and walked across to the bookcase. Running his fingers across a row of books he stopped and took out one book and walking towards the settee he said, 'You'll find this hard to believe I know, but I found this book on the floor. There was nothing else out of place in the room so it must've been this that fell, but goodness knows how, and until you mentioned Emma being a matchmaker I hadn't given it another thought.'

Dave handed the book to Angela and her eyes widened. 'This is a rare book, it's dated 1816!'

'I know' Dave said as he gestured towards the bookcase. 'And there are two more over there; the book is in three volumes.'

Angela very carefully turned a few of the delicate pages. Dave kissed the top of her head and went back to sifting through papers on the table. The ticking clock ticked on as both Angela and Dave became engrossed in the written word.

After a short while Angela replaced the book, but before doing so she gently removed the other two volumes of 'Emma' by Jane Austen. She reverently brushed her fingers over the covers before placing all three volumes on the bookshelf. She sighed and walked over to Dave who by this time had opened a number of envelopes, their contents' creases having been flattened and each one lying atop the other to one side of the table.

'How are you getting on?'

'Good. I think! Mum's letters to Lars are obviously not here except the one we've already seen dated June 1982, but he wrote to her quite a lot and it does look as though she kept them all at Grandma's. Thank goodness Grandma didn't get rid of them; we'd never have known the truth.'

'What d'you fancy for lunch?'

Dave smiled; 'You!'

Angela playfully punched Dave's shoulder. 'That'll do, Casanova. Let me put it another way, what food d'you fancy for lunch?'

'Let's go to town and have lunch. I think it's time I wrote to Lars so I could post a letter today and while we're in town we could check out a flight to Amsterdam, what d'you think? We could go over there for a few days during October half term and that would give us enough time to organise your workshop before we go.'

'Sounds like a plan; I'll take a shower and get dressed.'

'I think I'll join you' laughed Dave as he jumped up from his chair.

Chapter Seven

Cambridge UK

&

Bergen Amsterdam Netherlands

Local Information

Cambridge with its history and cobbled streets sits on the River Cam in the east of England and is home to its celebrated university. The university dates back to 1209 and includes King's College famed for its choir and towering Gothic chapel, Trinity College founded by Henry VIII and St John's College with its 16th century Great Gate. The university exhibits within its museums archaeology, anthropology, polar exploration and the history of science and zoology.

Shops in Cambridge cannot be explored hurriedly! A canny shopper takes time as there's a great deal to explore. In addition to the well-known stores there are fine independent boutiques and fashion warehouses, a seven day market and three shopping centres.

Angela's new fashion warehouse, as yet un-named, is located in the town centre. In addition to teaching general sewing techniques it will be a school of fashion and design for both adults and children, giving them the opportunity not only to develop additional sewing skills but to discover their own natural gift and ability to create designs. The window to Angela's shop at street level is housed below and to the front of her warehouse and will display her own fashion designs for children and women of all ages; these clothes will be on sale within her tastefully decorated store.

Dave and Angela worked tirelessly throughout the months of August, September and October, Dave arriving at the end of his working day from the beginning of his school autumn half-term to the completion of Angela's shop and warehouse. Their joint effort to adapt the building into an impressively eye-catching and modern fashion house and sewing school was a success, and they aimed for it to be ready to greet its clients and students within a short time of Angela and Dave returning from their Amsterdam trip at the end of October.

Angela insisted that when Cambridge City Football Club was playing at home Dave join Pete for a day away from the warehouse refurbishment, which of course both men were more than happy to arrange. Angela, Dave, Pete and Sandy spent many Saturday evenings in the now not-so-new Indian restaurant recapping on the ups and downs of their individual working weeks.

Cambridge Town football club was formed in 1908 as city status was not formally granted until 1951. The Milton Road site, which had been the club's home for ninety-one years, was redeveloped with the original iconic stadium being replaced by a business centre. A new ground was built directly behind the original which enabled the club to remain at the same site. However, planning permission was granted on the Milton Road site for housing development, and City's last game at Milton Road was in April 2013. Since City left Milton Road they have ground-shared at Histon and St Ives and this is where Dave and Pete watch City home matches. (*It is hoped the homeless and nomadic club will finally enjoy a new permanent stadium in the village of Sawston Cambridgeshire early 2022*).

Amsterdam is the capital of the Netherlands and known for its heritage, elaborate canal system and narrow houses with gabled facades which are the legacy of the city's 17th century Golden Age. The museum district contains the Van Gogh Museum, works by Rembrandt and Vermeer within the Rijksmuseum, plus modern art at the Stedelijk.

Lars lives in Bergen, a municipality and town in the Netherlands in the province of North Holland. The North Sea beaches make this area a popular destination for tourists.

Bergen has been the home to many painters, writers and architects. The Amsterdam School style of architecture provided fine building designs in other Dutch cities e.g. The Hague. Before retirement, Lars was a highly respected architect and many of his designs came to fruition within Amsterdam.

There are regular art fairs in Bergen as well as an annual music festival known as the Holland Music Sessions which takes place in August, and an arts festival in October named the Kunsttiendaagse. There is a nature area with the highest and widest dunes of the Netherlands; this is known as the Schoorlse Duinen and is a paradise for the nature lover. The seaside village of Bergen aan Zee holds an aquarium, and the Auto Union Museum in Bergen has a fine collection of classic cars.

Chapter Eight

Bergen Amsterdam

October 2019

The weekend of 19th and 20th October was a hectic one for Angela. In addition to the final flurry of emails from people looking to register on dressmaking courses, finalising a new contract with her business accountant and organising safety checks on the warehouse whilst she was away, she tripped over uneven paving! Dave drove her to hospital on Saturday where an x-ray confirmed a badly bruised and swollen ankle but, thankfully, no broken bones. Angela's left ankle was bandaged; she was provided with a crutch and pain relief and told to elevate the ankle as much as possible.

'Well that's going to be nigh on impossible' Angela cried as she peered over the shoulder of the Nurse to see Dave. She looked back to the nurse, 'and I have a plane to catch tomorrow.'

The nurse turned to Dave and suggested that when lying in bed he make certain his wife's left leg is raised on a couple of pillows, and whenever possible she should rest. Obviously his response was positive in that he would definitely make sure his *wife* rested and that her leg was raised whenever possible.

Angela's tears of frustration turned to tears of laughter as Dave, who'd taken on the facial expression of a Cheshire cat, helped her from the hospital bed and handed the crutch to her.

'Seriously, Dave; I'm going to ruin this trip now aren't I?'

'You couldn't ruin anything sweetheart. When we get to the airport I'll get a wheelchair for you and you know what that means don't you?'

'We'll be first on the plane?'

'Of course, and get off first, *and* get a buggy to the baggage hall, so don't feel bad, you're a VIP. Come on let's get you back to your mum's so you can finish packing.'

The 'Off Airport Meet & Greet' long-term parking area just a few minutes' walk from departures at London Heathrow Airport was Dave's choice for parking, and with the assistance of an airport vehicle he and Angela were checking in for their direct flight to Bergen within just ten minutes.

Once beyond security they headed for Starbucks Airside lounge; they ordered coffee and sandwiches to enjoy before their flight was called, and sat looking out at airplanes taking off from the runway. Dave put his hand over Angela's, gave her a loving smile and kissed her cheek before tucking in to his chicken sandwich. An hour later they were on board, and in a little under two hours they were landing at Bergen Flesland Airport.

Seated in a buggy its driver took them to the luggage area from where Dave ordered a taxi and, armed with a trolley and baggage with Angela hobbling alongside, he slowly entered the exquisite late afternoon sunshine of Bergen.

As arranged Dave phoned Lars to let him know they'd arrived and would meet with him the following day, which surprised Angela as she thought he would want to see Lars as soon as they arrived but, as a surprise, Dave had booked a one night stay at Hotel Zee Bergen.

Angela looked on bewildered. 'I thought Lars invited us to stay with him?'

'Well, this is our first night away together so it has to be special doesn't it?'

Dave's romantic gesture overwhelmed Angela and she hugged him. 'You continue to surprise me Mr Wilson.'

The taxi arrived and headed for Hotel Zee Bergen, a beautiful hotel set in the magnificent wooded area of Bergen Noord-Holland where Dave and Angela relaxed and enjoyed private moments away from home before setting off to spend a few days with Lars.

'Breakfast in bed in such beautiful surroundings is definitely something to remember isn't it?' Dave remarked as he rejoined Angela. 'Look at this breakfast! Scrambled eggs topped with smoked salmon and there's a pot of freshly brewed coffee and toast.'

'Ooh it smells delicious, I'm starving' Angela said as she positioned a pillow on the bed for the tray. 'What time are we leaving to meet Lars?'

'When we've eaten I'll give him a call and check.'

'I wonder what his house looks like; most houses in Amsterdam are colourful, terraced and with pointed apex roofs, although there are some very grand designs I believe.'

'Well, as Lars was an architect before he retired I should imagine he designed his own house and it'll be quite unique.'

The couple sat in silence as they ate looking out at the magnificent view through a window which stretched the whole of one wall. Angela turned to Dave and kissed his cheek.

'What was that for?'

'Thanks for organising everything Dave, and especially this hotel. It's such a shame my accident has stopped us from exploring the area.'

'We're together, and that's the main thing' Dave said as he gently kissed Angela's lips. 'And we're not here sightseeing; we'll be with Lars which will give me an opportunity to learn more about him.'

'He'll be about seventy won't he? He was a young man in the photos we saw; I wonder what he looks like now.'

Dave sighed. 'And Ann will be forty-seven. I'll bet she looks like Mum would have done had she lived to that age.'

'We'll soon find out.' Angela poured more coffee. 'Do you think we should've brought gifts for them, after all they're putting us up for a few days?'

Dave got out of bed and lifted a package from his suitcase. 'I thought I'd bring this for Ann.'

'What is it?'

'The '*Emma*' books; after all she's my Grandma's granddaughter and it seems only fitting don't you think?'

'That's a lovely idea; I hope she appreciates them. They must be worth a great deal of money by now.'

'Well, if she doesn't want them I'll take them back with me.'

Angela piled dishes onto the tray, got out of bed and placed the tray on the table by the window. 'We'd better get a move on' she said excitedly. 'I haven't got a plastic bag to put over my bandage so I'll take it off, and if my ankle's still swollen will you put the bandage back on for me?'

'Of course I will sweetheart. You seem to be walking better anyway.'

'I think the swelling's gone down a little; my ankle does feel a bit better this morning. I'll get showered while you phone Lars.'

'No I insist' Lars demanded, 'Marcus will pick you up at your hotel. What time will suit you?'

'Thank you Lars that's kind of you. We've just finished breakfast so, say in an hour?'

'Perfect. I'm really looking forward to meeting you David.'

Dave was smiling as he walked over to the bathroom and he called out to Angela.

'Lars is sending someone called Marcus to pick us up in an hour; maybe Marcus is Ann's husband.'

'Maybe, or maybe Lars married and Marcus is his son.'

'Oh, I never thought of that; there's a lot to find out isn't there?'

'Yes; now go away and let me get ready.'

'The weather's changed today so we should wear something warm I reckon.'

'That's okay, I've brought some cold weather clothes; now skoot!'

An hour later and the couple were standing under the hotel canopy with their suitcases awaiting the arrival of Marcus.

A black Tesla came to a stop directly in front of the hotel and a smartly dressed middle-aged man got out of the car. He held out his hand and introduced himself as Marcus. Once introductions were over, Marcus gestured to the couple that they get into the car whilst he put the luggage in the boot.

'I'll sit in the front' Dave said as he opened a rear door for Angela, taking the crutch to place in the boot.

The atmosphere within the car was a little tense although Marcus appeared to be trying to be friendly. He asked about the comfort of the flight from London and whether the couple would be sightseeing whilst in Bergen, to which Dave pointed out that Angela was still suffering a swollen ankle so walking far was not on their agenda. Dave felt this was not the time to enquire of Marcus as to his relationship with Lars.

There was little traffic unlike Cambridge, and within an hour the car entered a tree lined road leading to a wide, pale brick faced drive. Marcus brought the car to a stop in front of a very attractive and imposing residence having triangular rooflines and overhanging eves, the golden wooden frontage gleaming in the sunlight.

Having stepped out of the car Dave and Angela looked at each other in wonder. 'I've never seen a more beautiful house' Angela remarked. Dave nodded in agreement.

The couple stood facing the building admiring its many angles. Looking at the house from the front, its left roof slopes forward and down to rest above and overhang two wide wooden garage doors, the large wooden gallows bracket set to one side being an attractive feature. A hip roof dormer is set to the top of that roof and to its right is a gable fronted dormer, an extremely high angled window being its prominent feature. Below this stunning window and to its right the large square window gives a view to what is the only ground floor room to the front of the house. To the centre of the building, following the lines of its triangular rooflines, there is an architectural feature incorporating wide eves above an impressive front door and side glass panel all set upon a stone terrace. The terrace is laid to the remaining width of the building accessed by five wide and deep stone steps, all enhanced with ornate black iron rails. The overall effect of the building identifies a masterpiece of angular design.

'That must be Lars coming down the steps' Dave said to no-one in particular.

'It is' confirmed Marcus.

The couple walked towards Lars and saw a tall, slim and handsome man with short silver hair parted to one side. As they reached him they could see his face more clearly and saw feint lines branching out from his sea-blue eyes towards his temples, with deeper, longer lines creasing his cheeks. His face was pale and gaunt, and he held on to the handrail as he descended the steps.

As Lars reached the couple he gave them a wide welcoming smile and took hold of both Dave's hands in his. 'I'm so happy to see you in the flesh at last David' he said. He then looked over to Angela and embraced her saying 'You must be Angela. What a beautiful lady; David is such a lucky young man.'

Angela thanked Lars for having organised a car and for allowing her and Dave to stay with him at his home. She smiled towards Dave who was in control of the luggage, Marcus now driving the car towards one of the automatically opening garage doors.

'I should call your fiancé Dave not David then!' Lars quipped as he took hold of Angela's arm to assist her up the flight of steps, although in truth she was conscious of Lars being a little unsteady on his feet and she being the support for him.

Angela sighed, her inner self feeling welcomed and relaxed as she came to recognise Dave within Lars.

'Let me show you to your room first' Lars said as Dave and Angela entered the extensive hall, 'then I'll introduce you to Ingrid; you'll like her and especially the excellent meals she creates; I don't know what I'd do without her.'

Their room, on the ground floor to the side and towards the back of the house, gives a view to the garden through a wide, square bay window dressed with honey-coloured floor to ceiling curtains. It's a large room, painted pale blue with minimalist white furniture and a king size bed.

'Such a calming room' Angela remarked.

Lars suggested the couple unpack, refresh in their en suite and meet with him and Ingrid in the lounge when they're ready.

'What a lovely man' Angela said as they unpacked. 'And I wonder who Ingrid is?'

'Could be someone he pays to look after him; did you notice he doesn't look well?'

'Yes I did, and he struggled up those steps.'

'What do you think of Marcus?'

'I don't think I like him.'

'That's how I feel too; it's as though he's hiding something don't you think?'

'Definitely, but I can't put my finger on it because we don't know him. I'm suspicious of something though. Maybe we'll get a chance to work it out while we're here.'

'So, we've started our trip in suspicious mode! Are you Watson to my Sherlock?' Dave laughed.

'Of course I am, but I must freshen up. This house is absolutely gorgeous and Lars is a lovely gentleman, I can't wait to learn more about him.'

Chapter Nine

Ann and Emma Anderson

October 2019

Dave and Angela met with Lars and Ingrid in the lounge, Lars introducing Ingrid as one of his oldest friends whose husband worked alongside him for many years. He went on to say that since the death of her husband a few years ago Ingrid accepted his offer to be his companion and cook.

Ingrid held out her hand to Dave, 'so good to meet you, Lars tells me I should call you Dave not David which was the name we always used when speaking about you.'

Dave laughed. 'I hope you spoke well of me whatever you called me.'

'Of course we did' Ingrid laughed and turned towards Angela, 'but we've only recently found you Angela; what a lovely name for a beautiful lady. I'm sure we'll become friends even though we've only a few days to get to know each other. Come with me and I'll show you the kitchen; we can chat while I brew some tea.'

Alone with Lars, Dave wondered whether he should ask about Ann as no-one as yet mentioned her, but he saw Lars nervously shuffling in his seat and then he looked directly at Dave. 'You'll be wondering where my daughter is' he said.

'Yes. I thought she lived with you.'

'Ann lived here until her death in 2000.'

'I'm so sorry Lars; I didn't know.'

'Thank you. It was a great shock to us all; she would have been forty-seven this December. I miss her.'

Dave was finding this situation very awkward. Should he ask how Ann died? He said nothing and waited for Lars to continue.

The silence was broken by a young voice happily shouting, 'Are they here yet Grandpa?'

'That'll be my Granddaughter' Lars said with a beaming smile.

Dave stood frozen to the spot as a young lady, her blonde pony tail swishing about her head, came bounding into the room. When she eventually came to a stop by her grandfather's chair she smiled across to Dave saying excitedly 'You've *got* to be David! I can see that without being told, you're so like Grandpa! Well, like he was when he was younger' she laughed. Then she tapped Lars on the shoulders and kissed his cheek. 'There I told you, didn't I?' she said.

Lars laughed loudly. 'I wasn't going to bring that subject up yet, you young scamp!' He turned to Dave, 'This, as you can see, is Emma, my Granddaughter. Emma, this is Dave. We call him Dave now not David.'

Dave was literally dumbstruck! *Emma*?

'We'll talk later Dave' Lars said, 'there's so much you should know.'

Emma walked over to Dave and hugged him. 'I'm really glad you've come to stay with us, Uncle Dave' she said.

At that moment Angela walked in with Ingrid who was holding a tray of cups and biscuits.

'What's this?' Ingrid joked, 'you're not supposed to assault our guest Emma!'

As laughter filled the room, Angela's wide eyes sought Dave's.

Emma walked across to Angela and hugged her. 'You've got to be Angela' she said. 'Hi, I'm Emma. I'm so happy to meet you; please come sit with me.'

The family united in conversation and Emma was delighted to find Angela was a fashion designer as she herself was studying at Amsterdam's Fashion Institute, the only fashion institute in the Netherlands covering the entire fashion chain. Angela was excited to be able to talk about her craft and future aspirations with a like-minded female and the two women bonded immediately.

When conversations came to a natural and comfortable end, Lars said he would take a nap whilst Emma showed Dave and Angela around the house and its grounds, 'especially the memorial arch' he emphasized.

'Of course Grandpa' Emma said. 'Do you want me to explain?'

'Thank you my dear, yes I think you should.'

Emma took the tray of empty cups to the kitchen. Angela had abandoned the crutch, and although limping walked with her; they were still talking fashion.

When they returned to the lounge to join Dave, Emma announced, 'okay, let's start with the gardens, there's nothing much to see in the front but the back and side gardens are beautiful. Are you sure you're okay walking Angela?'

'I'll lean on Dave if I need to.'

Emma gestured to the back of the lounge, 'Follow me and we'll go through the patio doors to the deck and down the steps to the rear garden. The memorial garden is looking lovely even at this time of year Uncle Dave.'

In silence the trio walked on to the large wooden deck. The view was spectacular with trees to the boundaries, shaped lawns, a small pond and well stocked borders, although leaves were beginning to fall to the ground. Dave's eyes fell on a large stone structure beyond the pond.

As they reached the memorial garden it was obvious this was the resting place for Ann as a plaque bearing her name was set to one side of the arch, the abundant climbing peach coloured rose which adorned it still covered in flower. Angela's grip on Dave's hand tightened.

'I know this will come as a shock Uncle Dave' Emma said, 'but this is where my Mamma lies. Grandpa told me he couldn't leave her alone in a cemetery so he arranged for her to be buried here.'

Dave couldn't speak right away, but after a few minutes he looked to Emma. 'The plaque shows the dates 1972 to 2000, so Ann would have only been twenty-eight when she died?'

'That's right she died the day I was born.'

Angela couldn't hold back her shock, 'Oh my God, how awful; the family must have been devastated.'

Dave stared ahead and then to the ground below the arch. Emma put her hand on his arm, 'there's worse to come I'm afraid Uncle Dave' she said as she patted his arm. Tears welled in Dave's eyes.

'Mamma was being driven to hospital but the car veered off the road on ice and hit a tree.'

Dave took a sharp intake of breath. 'Oh my God' he choked.

Angela squeezed Dave's hand even tighter and asked, 'Was your father killed Emma?'

'Mamma wasn't married, and the man driving the car was Marcus. He survived.'

Dave spoke at last. 'Is Marcus your father?'

'No! Thank goodness. To be honest I don't like him, never have. His father was an old friend of Grandpa's and I'm told Marcus took on gardening and odd jobs for Grandpa when he lost his job about twenty years ago. He's a car mechanic and has a business of his own now, but Grandpa still asks him to help with tasks he can't manage, although I believe it took many years before he'd drive Grandpa's car again. Ingrid told me that Mamma had what she calls 'a bit of a fling' with Marcus when he first came here. When he is here I keep away from him. I'm not saying I blame him for Mamma's death, but there's something about that man that doesn't feel right to me. Does that make any sense?'

'Of course it does' Angela confirmed, 'he did seem rather unfriendly when he gave us a lift from the airport and wasn't keen to make conversation.'

'Grandpa doesn't speak about the accident and he's never referred to who my father might be so I've no idea what happened to him; he might be dead too for all I know. I tried to get information from Ingrid but all she would say was she never knew my father and that when Mamma came back home to live with Grandpa permanently she was pregnant with me; so my father's a mystery.'

Dave took in a deep breath. 'What you're telling me is hard to take in Emma. Do you know that my mother died in a road accident too?'

'Yes, Grandpa told me, and he wrote to your grandmother. Did you know he'd written?'

'I did, but only recently and that's another chapter in the story which I'll talk to you and your Grandpa about later.'

'Grandpa always knew you were his son you know?'

'I've only just worked that out for myself Emma; I wish I'd known earlier I could have visited long before now.'

Emma hugged Dave. 'You're here now Uncle Dave, that's all that matters.'

Emma, Dave and Angela continued their walk around the gardens, stopping to look at particularly outstanding areas such as the masses of purple Verbena growing either side of steps leading to another section of the garden. Once the gardens were explored Emma led the couple back to the house where she proudly showed off her Grandpa's architectural skills.

Lars recovered sufficiently to be a very genial host at dinner, a meal which Ingrid prepared with exceptional attention to detail. He raised his glass of wine to celebrate having his son with him at last, saying he'd arranged a DNA test to allay any misconceptions. Angela was sitting to one side of Dave, and Emma the other, and both women leaned towards Dave and kissed him on the cheek. Ingrid laughed saying she wished she'd had her camera to which Emma shrieked 'I'll get mine.'

When Emma returned she gave the camera to Ingrid and the two women once again took up their positions and kissed Dave to the great amusement of Lars.

Once recovered from this highly emotional show of affection Dave raised his glass, 'To Lars, a man I've only now come to recognise as my father, a man who has changed my life for the better; thank you.'

A cheer went up around the table and when it died down Dave raised his glass again. 'And, not forgetting my newly found niece. What a beautiful lady, and she has my Grandma's name, Emma. This has to be the best day of my life. Cheers!'

Chapter Ten

Marcus

October 2019

The days are passing far too quickly for everyone.

By Tuesday evening Dave's mind is again being drawn to why Marcus has visited a couple of times and yet appears only to be checking on how Lars is feeling, leaving the house after only half an hour or so. This worries Dave as he's not aware of Lars having a serious illness, although he doesn't look very well. As he's still trying to make sense of this anomaly Dave decides not to talk to Lars about it but does talk at length with Angela who agrees to broach the subject of Marcus with Ingrid.

Lars was too unwell to eat breakfast on Wednesday and stayed in his room. Emma was so concerned she insisted on phoning the doctor to request a visit. He arrived within the hour and diagnosed gastroenteritis, leaving a prescription and suggesting Lars rest and that he drink plenty of water throughout the day. Lars felt weak and so didn't object, and this quite sudden change in his health worried Dave who was happy to collect the medication for him, but Emma heard the conversation and insisted she get her car and drive him into town, which was a relief to Dave as he realised he had no idea where the pharmacy was.

Rain was falling heavily so it was definitely a day to stay indoors, and this gave Angela an opportunity to help Ingrid in the kitchen and seek her opinion of Marcus. Once conversation about Lars becoming unwell, debates on if and when the rain would stop, and how lovely it was to see Emma so keen to go into town with her uncle came to their natural end, Angela asked Ingrid if Marcus often came to the house.

'To be absolutely honest I've no idea why he's been coming here so much lately, especially as Lars hasn't asked him to do anything for him for a while, but since Lars told him about your visit and asked him if he had time to pick you up at the airport he's been coming over almost daily. Maybe he likes you!' Ingrid laughed.

'Oh God I hope not!' Angela said with a screech to her voice. She deliberately brought Ann's pregnancy into the conversation and found that Marcus was a constant visitor to the house at that time.

'He seemed different then and he and Ann seemed to get on well.'

'Could he be Emma's father?'

'Oh no, he definitely wasn't Ann's type in *that* way. She was very secretive about the father but if it was Marcus I'm sure Lars would have made an effort to keep him involved with his daughter. No, Marcus has shown no paternal interest in Emma since the day she was born.'

Angela carefully ventured further. 'Ann lived away from home while at university did she?'

'That's right. Lars never felt she was truly happy but of course she was a grown woman and, although Lars did try to guide her, he felt she was unable for some reason to find her true vocation. She did get into Amsterdam's University of Art but then moved to the Academy of Music and Dance and didn't go on to theatre which would have been a natural progression. Poor Ann, she always seemed lost somehow. Lars was heartbroken when she died and his life seemed to fall apart, but of course she left him Emma and she's brought a great deal of happiness to this house and everyone who visits.'

'So,' Angela ventured, 'Ann lived away from home for quite a number of years then?'

'Once she left university she worked in various boutiques in Amsterdam and flat shared with a group of young people. She married one of them and I've since found out he was a brute! She didn't tell her father until her divorce when she also changed her name back to Anderson. Of course Lars was upset to find she'd kept her marriage a secret until then, but he was delighted she wanted to come back home. That would have been early summer, and Emma was born the following March.'

'Do you think Ann's health was affected by her mother's death?'

'Definitely, and of course she remembered her mother even though she was very young when Sara left for England. She always hoped her mother would come back, and sometimes when visiting I'd see her staring out the lounge window probably picturing her mother walking up the drive and not me. Sara did come back a few times but only because her newspaper wanted her to be in Amsterdam for one or two pieces for the paper, her being a journalist of course, but she always returned to England. Then, not long after being told her mother was definitely coming to live here for good Lars had to tell Ann her mother had died. Ann was broken-hearted. So, yes, Sara's death affected Ann, in fact even though I felt sorry for Sara being married to a man who obviously mistreated her, I could never completely forgive her for leaving her daughter in the first place. Lars couldn't have loved his daughter more but she became what you call...' Ingrid hesitated, 'a rebel, I'm afraid.'

Angela sighed heavily. 'You know, don't you, that Dave and I found letters from Lars to Sara which his grandmother kept hidden for years? It's clear from them Sara was a lost soul searching for the right thing to do but hesitating and sometimes taking a wrong turn, but it was obvious she loved Lars and Ann.'

Ingrid looked up from peeling vegetables, a downhearted look in her eyes and, after a moment's hesitation she said, 'Ann was a lost soul too, so I hope it doesn't run in the family!'

'There's no doubt Emma is a bright star and she obviously takes after her Grandpa, and maybe there's a little bit of her Uncle Dave in her too!'

'Oh that would be such a good thing' Ingrid said excitedly. 'Dave has a kind and loving character and knows exactly where he's heading. Talking of Dave, have you set a date yet?'

Angela's smile broadened. 'We've only recently rekindled our friendship Ingrid, but if he asked me to marry him tomorrow I reckon I'd say yes! But please don't tell him I said that!'

The two women laughed out loud, but Angela was acutely aware they'd moved away from talking about Marcus, so swiftly brought him back into the conversation.

'You say Marcus is coming here more often lately. Does he sit with Lars or do odd jobs while he's here?'

'There haven't been many jobs for him to do for a long time' Ingrid said. 'Lars needed someone to pick you up from the airport otherwise I doubt we'd have seen him this side of Christmas. He doesn't sit for long with Lars but he likes to pour him an aperitif before dinner or cup of sweet tea before he leaves.'

'Do you make up the tea or does Marcus?'

'Sometimes he insists I sit down and it's the least he can do to help, so I suppose I take advantage of him don't I?'

Angela continued to prepare the vegetables with Ingrid, her mind now conjuring up a picture of Marcus she'd rather not have imagined.

When alone with Dave in their room Angela told him of her revealing conversation with Ingrid, putting more emphasis on Ingrid's dislike of Marcus.

'D'you know what, I think I've worked it out!' Angela said excitedly.

'I'm ahead of you Watson, Marcus is a car mechanic isn't he? I'm no medic but I reckon he might be trying to poison Lars with antifreeze!'

'No! Surely not! Why would he want to do *that*? I thought maybe he's trying to put himself in front of you as far as Lars' affection is concerned, not *kill* him!'

'Think it through Watson. When Lars dies everything he has will pass to Emma won't it? And if Emma were to die...?'

'But Marcus isn't Emma's father so he can't inherit on her death.'

'What if he *is* her father?'

'Then everything goes to him! Oh my God, you could be right.'

'He might have kept himself out of the picture initially so he didn't have to pay maintenance for the child. After all, apparently Ann never divulged the name of the father so he was on a safe wicket there.'

Angela breathed out noisily, 'It does look as though history repeated itself with Marcus driving into a tree and killing Ann.'

'But Mum wasn't pregnant when she died.'

'I know, but if Barry who you thought was your father deliberately drove his motorbike into a tree to kill Sara because he found out she was going to leave him for Lars, isn't it a twist of fate that Sara's daughter Ann died in a car Marcus was driving? Maybe they'd rowed about who was the father of the baby and he was going to kill all of them in the accident. That's really bizarre. The main difference is that Marcus survived where Barry didn't.'

'*Exactly*, Marcus survived and has apparently helped Lars over the years, and of course that way he's been keeping himself involved with the family.'

'And now *you've* turned up! Surely you'd be entitled to inherit as Lars' son? He must be trying to do the deed before Lars can prove you're his son or make a Will to include you. What can we do? Not that you're thinking of any inheritance, you're not that type, but we'll have to help Lars won't we?'

'If the DNA test I took the other day proves I am Lars' son, and I'm assuming it will then it's too late for Marcus even if Lars dies. If he turns up tonight I'll keep my eyes on him. If he is trying to kill off Lars he's been going about it slowly otherwise it would be too obvious. That can only mean he's putting very small amounts of something in the night time drink he sometimes prepares, and as Lars is unwell it's not likely to be alcohol tonight but tea.'

'What should *I* do?'

'If he goes into the kitchen on his own you go in and say you'll help him because everyone wants tea. Make sure the bowl of sugar is on the tray as usual and see if he keeps Lars' cup separate to the others and puts extra sugar in that cup. When you're back in the lounge see which cup he gives Lars and if it's the one he put the sugar in say that's mine as you saw he'd already put extra sugar in it. Say you've noticed Lars doesn't like too much sugar but I've got a very sweet tooth. That should shake him. He'll have put extra sugar in the cup to cover any taste of antifreeze.'

'Then what; you can't drink it if it's poisoned!'

'I won't drink it I'll keep talking and hold on to the cup while you watch Marcus' expression. If we're right there'll be antifreeze in it as well as sugar. Then tomorrow we'll tell the Police what we suspect and have them get the tea analysed. Ethylene glycol and methanol are poisonous and it doesn't take much antifreeze to poison someone so we'd better get this right and *quick*!'

'If this wasn't so serious it'd be exciting.'

'Very true Watson. I reckon we make a good team, don't you?'

Angela nodded and tried to hold back a smile as she reminded herself of her conversation with Ingrid.

'Yes I agree Sherlock. It's time for us to ruin Marcus' plan so let's go get him!'

Chapter Eleven

The Will

October 2019

Marcus did turn up on Wednesday at around seven o'clock saying he called in to see how Dave and Angela were enjoying their time in Bergen, but when he found Lars was already in bed he left almost immediately.

Angela turned to face Dave, 'Well, that didn't work.'

'Tomorrow's another day; our plans are on hold that's all. It's a bit obvious though, don't you think?'

'Are we reading too much into this?'

'No! I reckon his attitude tonight only confirms he's up to something. He's just too stupid to realise we can read him like a book.'

Dinner was late as Ingrid held it back in the hope Lars would feel hungry after yet another long sleep. She took him a bowl of vegetable soup and when she came back into the dining room it was obvious she felt relieved. 'He's sitting up and wants to eat his soup!' she said with a smile.

Later that evening Lars came downstairs and sat with the family apologising for not being with Dave and Angela at dinner when they only have a few days left to be with him. During the family conversations Lars admitted his recent illness brought him to consider his future.

Lars looked directly at Dave, 'I've made arrangements for my Solicitor to see me tomorrow as I want to update my Will to include you, and he's agreed to come to the house.'

That decision astonished Dave and he tried to dissuade Lars from including him which would take a portion of inheritance from his granddaughter.

Emma jumped up from her chair and knelt before Lars.

'Grandpa's already spoken to me and I agree with him that as his son you are entitled to inherit. I'm really happy to have found you too Uncle Dave, and by the way you're nineteen birthdays and Christmases in debt to me!'

The evening continued in jovial conversation but was brought to an end when Lars admitted he could stay up no longer, although he insisted he was happier than he'd been in many years because now he has all his family around him.

'I'm hoping to feel much better tomorrow Son and spend more time with you, and of course you too Angela.'

Emma said goodnight and kissed everyone three times, as is the tradition in the Netherlands, and when she was kissing her Grandpa he whispered something to her. When she reached Angela she whispered, 'Make sure Uncle Dave kisses you three times *every* night. Remember what I told you?'

'Oh I *will* Emma!'

Lars and Emma were still whispering, turning to look back at Dave and laughing as they left the lounge to go to their respective rooms.

Dave scratched his head and shouted 'What's going on?'

Emma turned back, peeped around the door and with a beaming smile announced 'You'll soon find out Uncle Dave!'

Angela took hold of Dave's hand and led him to their room at the back of the house. 'Okay, things are going to have to change Sherlock!'

'What on earth d'you mean?'

'Well, as you're now officially acknowledged as the son of Lars you'll have to follow at least some of his country's traditions while you're here, so let's start with hello goodbye or goodnight to family and friends shall we?'

Dave sat on the edge of the bed. 'Go on then' he said, 'I'm your friend so show me how to say goodnight.'

'Are you ready for this?'

By now Dave was laughing too. 'Well, I *think* I am, but I'll let you know later.'

Angela took off her dress and walked over to Dave who was still sitting on the edge of the bed. She kissed him gently on his right cheek. Then she moved away a little and took off her bra before returning to Dave to kiss him gently on his left cheek, allowing her breast to touch his shoulder. By this time Dave was becoming a little uncomfortable!

'How long does it take to say goodnight here?'

'Not long now.'

Returning to Dave for a third kiss, this time on his right cheek once more, Angela was naked.

Dave reached out for Angela's hand. 'No wonder the population here is on the rise' he laughed, 'now it's my turn but I don't think I'll manage to reach three!'

Although Lars came down for breakfast he didn't eat but did have coffee and conversation with his family. Thursday was the day of his appointment to update his Will, and Mr Hyam agreed to come to the house late morning. Dave still felt uncomfortable but consoled himself with the fact the family were, as one, insistent changing his Will was the prerogative of Lars and only Lars.

When Mr Hyam arrived at the house Dave and Angela accepted Ingrid's suggestion they should cut a few flowers from the garden and visit Ann's grave. With secateurs in one hand and Dave's hand in the other Angela walked through the garden in silence. She cut white daisies and purple verbena while Dave stood and watched, recalling the day they found each other over his grandmother's gate, and a sudden urge to hold Angela aroused him.

Recent rain had filled the vase on Ann's marble gravestone so Angela used the water Dave brought with him to wash away leaves which had fallen on top and around the stone. She arranged the flowers and as Dave watched her his tears welled. He wondered how different life would have been if only he'd had the chance to meet his sister in life. After a few minutes Angela stood at Dave's side and held his hand; they both bowed their heads in silent prayer.

'I love you Miss Thomas' Dave whispered as they turned to walk back to the house.

'I love you too Mr Wilson'.

Having walked around the garden arm in arm admiring its late autumn colours, Dave and Angela sat on the wrought iron seat by the pond. They didn't speak but leaned their bodies against each other, holding hands and simply breathing in the tranquil atmosphere.

After a few minutes Dave tapped Angela's hand. 'C'mon, I suppose we should get back to the house.'

'Hopefully Mr Hyam's gone now. We've been out for more than an hour and my feet are cold.'

'If he's still there we can always go to our room, and Ingrid's keen on trying to get Lars to eat so she's probably sorting lunch as we speak. You know, I'm still a bit uncomfortable about being in the Will, after all I didn't know Lars until last weekend.'

'But you're his son and he wants to acknowledge that. He's a very generous man who wants to do the right thing by you. Will you change your name to Anderson now you know for sure Lars is your father?'

'I never thought of that. Do you think I should?'

'Better check with Lars. He's probably put you in his Will as Wilson but there's time before the Will is written up and signed.'

'I'll have a private word with him later. And that reminds me Marcus might come over tonight so we'll have to put our plan into action if he does.'

When Dave and Angela reached the house there was no one in the lounge and everywhere was quiet, but the smell of food greeted them. They walked into the kitchen and saw Ingrid preparing lunch, but as she was deep in thought she didn't hear or see them.

Crossing over to the Aga Angela said quietly, 'The smell of food cooking is making me hungry.'

Ingrid jumped in surprise at Angela's voice close behind her. 'Oh! I didn't hear you come in. Lars has gone up to his room but promised to come down for lunch. In fact, Dave, maybe you would go up and let him know lunch will be in about twenty minutes; is that okay?'

'Of course Ingrid that's no problem. I want to ask him something anyway.'

Dave kissed Angela on the cheek and left the room.

'Can I help you with anything Ingrid?'

'You could set the table dear that would be a help. The bowls and cutlery are on the side over there' Ingrid said nodding to the extended work surface.

Angela completed setting the table as Dave came into the dining room with Lars. They were both smiling as they sat down and Dave was the first to speak.

'Lars is ahead of me, his Solicitor's organising a change of name deed for tomorrow! That's efficiency for you isn't it?'

Angela smiled and turned to Lars. '*I'll say*!'

Lars tapped the table 'Well, it will prevent any problems in the future but Dave will have to organise changing account names and the like when he gets back to England. Ah! Here comes Ingrid and lunch, and I actually feel like eating today.'

Ingrid placed bowls of risotto in front of Dave and Angela before returning to the kitchen to bring in the remaining food. 'Let me help you' Angela shouted after her.

'No it's fine dear, I can manage.'

'Where's Emma?' asked Lars. 'I've just realised she's not at home.'

Ingrid shouted from the kitchen that Emma had a phone call from a friend who wanted to meet her in town for lunch but she'd be back in time for dinner.

When Ingrid returned to the dining room holding two more bowls of risotto she asked Dave why he'd given Lars his bowl of food.

Dave wasn't certain, but he felt he'd been told off! 'Lars said he really felt like eating today so I thought I'd let him get a head start' he stuttered.

Ingrid took the bowl away from Lars and placed it once again in front of Dave, her brow wrinkling. 'Lars loves his champignon, so he gets a little extra.'

Lars rubbed his hands together. 'Oh yes, and at this time of year there are many champignon to choose from. Tuck in and enjoy.'

The mushroom risotto was indeed delicious and both Dave and Angela complimented Ingrid on her very tasty lunch.

Angela helped Ingrid clear the lunch dishes. Lars was interested in knowing as much as possible about Dave's life with his grandmother, his friends and how he came to meet up again with Angela. They were both laughing when Ingrid and Angela walked back into the room.

'Can we join in the fun?' Angela asked with a laugh, deliberately searching out Dave's eyes.

'I was just telling Lars how we went about extracting Grandma's note from her chair and the positions we ended up in.'

'You should tell him about your grandmother moving things too.'

Ingrid's eyes widened. 'What's that? But your grandmother died!'

Dave looked heavenwards, 'It seems passing over to the other side hasn't stopped Grandma from keeping in touch with me.'

'Whatever did she do?' Ingrid asked.

'She moved her chair and put the box full of letters on top; we think to make sure we looked at them.' Dave looked over to Lars. 'That's where we found your letters.'

Ingrid's eyes widened. 'Oh my, are you sure they were moved?'

Angela explained where the chair and box were the night before and where they were found the next morning. 'It could only have been Dave's grandmother who moved them but it's not scary, although I did jump when a book fell off the bookshelf!'

Lars and Ingrid gulped and looked at each other.

'It's true!' Dave said laughing. 'And best of all, *I* think anyway, is how Grandma worked her magic to cause me to meet up with Angela again.'

Lars smiled and his face lit up. 'That's wonderful! Death hasn't stopped her from looking after you, and I'll bet she'll be with you wherever you go.'

Angela laughed too. 'I've no problem with that so long as she stops dropping books on the floor!'

The afternoon was passing in pleasant conversation, and when Emma joined the family the atmosphere lifted to yet another level with more fun and laughter.

'How d'you fancy coming into town with me Angela? We could look around the fashion boutiques and that might give you some ideas for your business. There's plenty of time before dinner.'

'I'd love that provided Dave and Lars don't mind me disappearing!'

Lars was excited to think his granddaughter and Angela had so much in common and got on so well, and told them he thought it was a great idea they were shopping together.

'Why don't you buy a pretty dress for yourself Angela? Then you'll have an authentic Dutch fashion piece to take home.'

Emma clapped her hands with delight, 'that's a great idea Grandpa. Let's go Angela!'

Angela and Emma returned to the house at the end of the day, Angela remarking on how beautiful the building looked with lights inside and out emphasizing its various attractive lines.

The two women danced up the steps, Angela a little slower than Emma, with multiple boutique shopping bags flying about in the air around them, entering the house bringing excitement in with them.

'We're home!' shrieked Emma, 'and we've emptied the Fresh Pepper boutique! We'll give you all a fashion show after dinner if you're lucky.'

Dave shouted from the lounge, 'I'll *definitely* look forward to that, but don't forget our plan Angela!'

'Let's go to your room and separate our purchases' Emma said, 'and you can tell me what Dave's plan is, it sounds exciting!'

Angela was stumped! Possible scenarios raced around in her head, but all she could come up with was, 'Oh he's always thinking up a plan for something and to be honest they're never that exciting!'

Chapter Twelve

The Ring

October 2019

Lars felt well enough to eat dinner, helped no doubt by the aromas seeping into the lounge from the kitchen. He got up from his armchair and walked over to the drinks cabinet. He turned to look back at Dave.

'I apologise for my lack of consideration Dave. Alcohol hasn't been on my mind this week as you can imagine, but I should have thought that you and Angela might have liked a drink. Would you like to try this?' He held up a stone-like straight sided bottle. 'It's *jenever*, spelt with a jay but sounds like yenever; it's a Dutch spirit quite like whisky. We have this young jenever as an aperitif, and if you like it I also have *old* jenever, a digestif which you can try later.'

'That sounds great thanks Lars I'd love to try something unique to the Netherlands, and to be honest until now I haven't thought of alcohol either so please don't apologise.'

'There's a selection of drinks here so don't let me forget to offer Angela something will you?'

Both men sat for a moment sipping their drinks in quiet contemplation when Lars shifted in his chair and took a small box from his trouser pocket. Dave looked on intrigued. Lars held the red velvet box in his right hand, staring at it for what seemed longer than the moment it actually was before he spoke.

'It's obvious you and Angela are very happy together but she doesn't wear an engagement ring. Do you intend to marry her? I hope so, and I hope you don't wait too long as you never know how long you might have together.'

Dave's throat tightened. 'I don't want to lose her that's for sure, but I'm afraid to pop the question; she did say a while ago she thinks she's been put off men for life!'

'Don't be afraid Son; I lost the love of my life, don't lose yours!'

Still cradling the box Lars turned it around in the palm of his hand, caressing it with each turn. Then he leaned forward.

'Here take this it will make me so happy to see Angela wearing it.'

Dave held the box and looked over to Lars. 'Are you sure you want me to take this?'

Tears were welling in Lars' eyes. 'It should have been on your mother's finger so it's only fitting it should go to you.'

When Dave opened the box he found himself speechless. He gently touched the square ruby surrounded by tiny diamonds and then ran his fingers across the two larger diamonds set either side as shoulders on a platinum ring.

Lars smiled. 'Yes,' he said, 'it is exquisite isn't it?'

'It must have cost a fortune!'

'It did, but don't let that stop you from accepting it. I've talked generally about precious stones with Emma and she's a diamonds only lady so she won't be upset I've passed the ring to you.'

'That makes me feel better. I wouldn't want to upset Emma.'

'So when do you intend to propose?'

Gosh! You've taken me by surprise Lars. I'm not sure.'

'Your last night with us is Saturday and if it's not too much to ask, is there any chance you can place it on Angela's finger before you leave us? You only have two days left!' Lars said with an obvious twinkle in his eyes.

Before he had a chance to answer the sound of laughter entered the room. Dave put the box into his trouser pocket just as Angela and Emma bounced into the room wearing their boutique purchases. The two women walked across the room imitating models on a catwalk, causing the men to raise their glasses as they cheered.

The fashion show was a great success, and once the ladies regrouped it was almost time for dinner. Lars remembered to offer Angela an aperitif and both she and Emma chose Gin and tonic.

Chapter Thirteen

Wild Mushrooms

October 2019

Ingrid came into the lounge with Marcus, but she returned to the kitchen leaving him standing in the doorway. Dave's eyes met Angela's.

Lars offered Marcus a drink but he refused saying he was meeting up with a friend and wouldn't be staying more than a few minutes.

'I'm glad to see you're looking better Lars' Marcus remarked. 'Dave and Angela's visit has been a tonic for you hasn't it? I've been worried about you lately but I see you've got a drink already so you're obviously feeling better. I'll just say goodnight to Ingrid and then I'll go; sorry to have disturbed your evening everyone.'

Marcus headed for the kitchen. Angela waited a moment before following him.

Dave wondered whether he should go too, but that would leave Lars and Emma drinking alone and it would look suspicious if he jumped up to follow Angela, so he started up a conversation asking when it was that Lars began to feel unwell. Lars said he'd been quite healthy for an *almost* seventy year old until a few weeks ago when he fell ill with a stomach virus he doesn't seem to be able to shake off.

'It's no fun getting old Son so enjoy life as much as you can while you can. As I've said, you never know what's around the corner.'

In the kitchen Marcus was admiring Ingrid's cooking skills and asking how her stew smelled so much better than anything he could conjure up. He looked up and saw Angela before Ingrid had time to speak.

'I was just saying to Ingrid I reckon she must have a secret ingredient for her stew as mine never smells this good.'

'It does smell delicious' Angela answered, 'Ingrid is certainly an expert when it comes to cooking; we've had delicious meals this week and I've picked up a few hints from her too.'

Ingrid smiled but said nothing.

Marcus turned to Angela as he pointed to the pot on the hob, 'This is Hachee, it's what we in the Netherlands call our beef stew.'

'My English beef stew never smells this good; you'll have to give me that recipe too Ingrid.'

'Of course I will' Ingrid said. 'Now, Marcus, are you staying for dinner; there's enough for one more or are you going? If you're going, then please leave me to get on!'

Marcus leaned across the worktop and moved a small white bowl with his hand. 'This looks interesting' he said. What is it?'

'Are you going or not?' Ingrid said angrily as she took hold of the small bowl.

Angela felt uneasy. The atmosphere, although on the surface amiable, felt a little strained. Ingrid put down the bowl and flung her arms up high asking them both to leave her kitchen, but before they did Marcus once again picked up the small white bowl.

'I think you've got a secret ingredient here Ingrid!' Marcus said as he sniffed the brown mousse-like mixture. He held it out to Angela asking her what she thought it smelt like.

'Mushrooms I think.'

Ingrid was livid! 'This kitchen is my domain' she shouted, 'and what I do in here is my business; now *leave*, both of you.'

Angela was dumbstruck. She'd never seen this side of Ingrid's character and it frightened her a little. Marcus was still holding the white bowl as he stared at Ingrid.

Dave, Lars and Emma heard Ingrid shouting. They walked quickly into the kitchen to see her lurching towards Marcus to retrieve the bowl. The scene caused Dave to move forward and quietly ask Marcus to give the bowl to him.

'Check the contents!' Marcus pleaded as he handed the bowl to Dave.

Lars leaned against the door to the kitchen his head in his hands, his body slowly falling to the floor. Marcus ran to Lars and helped him to the lounge where he sat comforting him.

'What's going on?' Lars whispered.

'Emma's phoning 112 so the Politie should be here very soon. Don't worry Lars you're safe now.'

Chapter Fourteen

Ingrid

October 2019

The Police arrived to find Ingrid sitting on a kitchen chair, Emma and Angela keeping her there with their hands on her shoulders. Ingrid's look was sinister, her brow deeply furrowed. She said nothing other than to confirm who she was when asked by the Police.

Dave handed the small white bowl to the policeman who was in charge.

'Lars has been unwell for a few weeks now and Marcus was concerned for his health so he's been checking on him' Dave said. 'He'll tell you more of course but you should definitely get this mixture analysed. It smells like mushrooms and we're certain Ingrid was about to put that into the bowl of stew for Lars, leaving the rest of us with just the stew. I've noticed most of the meals she prepared this week contained mushrooms and she made sure Lars got a bowl containing extra mushrooms because, she said, he really likes them.'

Ingrid squirmed her way out of the hold Emma and Angela had on her but one of the policemen grabbed her by the arm, keeping her back from the block of knives she was trying to reach. Emma screamed and fell into Angela's open arms.

Ingrid turned to Emma, a look of evil in her eyes and sheer venom in her voice, 'Who's been looking after Lars for years?' she yelled, 'Me! And then those two turn up! *Son* indeed! And where does that leave us?'

Angela found it hard to stay silent as Emma wept. 'It's hard to believe you could be so evil after all this family's done for you' she shouted to Ingrid, 'you're not married to Lars so how would Dave being his son affect *you*? You have *no* rights!'

Ingrid's look darkened but she didn't get chance to comment as she was immediately handcuffed and taken out of the house by the police.

Dave, Angela and Emma joined Lars and Marcus in the lounge. Ingrid was escorted to a Police car and within minutes the convoy of cars left the property. Had Ingrid looked up to the lounge window she would have seen a row of people holding on to one-another in shock at what they had witnessed.

Emma immediately called the family doctor who arranged for Lars to be taken into hospital for tests and remedial treatment to ensure he would recover from what appeared to be a series of poisoned meals over a number of days.

Analysis of the suspect mixture revealed it held more than one of the Netherland's poisonous mushrooms.

A police detective called to the house on Friday morning to give Lars an update and confirm Ingrid had been arrested on a charge of attempted murder. Emma said she'd pass on the message as her grandfather was in hospital but would be home on Saturday if he'd like to come back.

'May I take your name?' The detective asked.

'Of course, I'm Emma Anderson; Lars Anderson's granddaughter.'

'If you need to get in touch with me my name's Fredrik Janssen, and here's my card just in case there's a change to when your grandfather leaves hospital. It's good he's being looked after in hospital as you can never tell how a person might react to poisonous mushrooms, but I'm surprised he's being discharged so soon.'

'You don't know my grandfather! He insisted he'd recovered sufficiently from his ordeal to spend time with his son before he returns to England on Sunday, so the hospital staff had no choice but to discharge him otherwise he would have just got up from his bed and walked out.'

'Under the circumstances maybe it would be better if I call back on Monday.'

'Thank you, that's very considerate of you. I'll contact you if there's any change.'

Closing the front door Emma turned to Angela, 'Phew! What a good looking guy! I'll have to make sure I'm here on Monday *and* looking good! Maybe I'll drip feed information so he'll have to keep coming back for more!' she laughed.

'You always look good Emma' Angela laughed, 'you'll have to keep me updated as to how you get on with your handsome detective! Do you promise?'

'Oh I promise. I've got a good feeling about him. Mmm delicious! He's got a great looking body that's for sure, don't you think so?'

'You're definitely your Uncle Dave's niece!' Angela laughed.

Emma stood looking out the lounge window watching the detective get into his car, but before he did he turned and looked up to the window, giving Emma a wide smile.

'Wow! He looked back to see me and smiled; did you see that? Roll on Monday!'

Immediately the detective's car had gone, Dave and Angela left to visit Lars leaving Emma to the peace of the house and thoughts of once again seeing DI. Fredrik Janssen.

The doorbell rang and Emma found Marcus standing on the step smiling and holding a bouquet of flowers in each hand.

'Come on in Marcus. What beautiful flowers!'

'They're for you and Angela. You've been through a lot this past week with one thing and another.'

'Angela's with Uncle Dave visiting Grandpa, but let me take the flowers and put them in a bucket of water 'till she gets back. Ooh they're gorgeous, thank you.'

Emma gave Marcus an affectionate thank you kiss on the cheek and offered him a cup of coffee which he accepted; they sat together in the kitchen.

'I'm so sorry I misjudged you Marcus' Emma said softly, 'obviously I didn't realise you were suspicious of Ingrid and were especially worried about Grandpa's recent illness. I just thought you were a miserable guy!'

Marcus laughed. 'That's understandable, but I couldn't get the police involved until I had more to go on. I've always thought Ingrid was too keen to make herself at home here even though she has a home of her own not far from here, and she has a son.'

'Really, I don't remember her ever talking about a son!'

'Yes, his name is Baz; he'd be about 47 now I think. He got married and moved to America with his American wife and hasn't been back to see his mother since he left twenty years ago. I think Ingrid wondered if he was your father as he did date Ann when she was here. If I remember there was a big fall out after his father died and he hasn't spoken to his mother since.'

'Do you think Ingrid is jealous of Dave? She certainly sounded annoyed that he suddenly turned up and Lars accepted him as his son.'

'Yes definitely. I've dropped by as often as possible since Lars took to his bed during the day because it's not like him. I realise now it wasn't long after he got Dave's letter and invited him to come here that Ingrid started to put her poisonous plan into practice. I got suspicious of her about a year ago when she was acting as if she owned the place, and I reckon she'd been working on getting Lars to marry her but that obviously failed, and then when Lars acknowledged Dave as his son she must have been livid. That's when I was certain she was trying to harm him but I couldn't work out how, then one day I thought I saw her put something in his bowl of soup so I called round as often as I could after that hoping to confirm what I suspected. I have to admit though I didn't think it would be mushrooms even though the papers recently reported an abundance of poison mushrooms and holidaymakers picking the wrong ones, but of course Ingrid would definitely know the difference.'

'Maybe that's where she got the idea from.'

'You're probably right.'

Lars had given Dave a key to the house so he was able to let himself in when he returned from the hospital.

Marcus stood when Angela walked into the lounge. 'Emma tells me Lars is expecting to be discharged later today so I'll drive over and pick him up.' He looked back to Emma and asked if she'd like to go with him.

'Yes, thanks Marcus I would.'

Dave walked over to Marcus holding out his hand in friendship. 'I'm really sorry I feel I should admit I was worried it was you trying to poison Lars.'

'Me too' added Angela. 'I thought you were unfriendly when I first met you, but now I can see you were probably deep in thought because you were worried about Lars. Obviously you couldn't divulge your fears to us as we were complete strangers.'

Marcus pushed his left hand through his hair and laughed. 'Well, you didn't know me from Adam when I picked you up at the airport; it was impossible for me to start telling you about my suspicions so it was best to say nothing.'

'Oh Angela I nearly forgot' Emma said excitedly, 'Marcus brought each of us a bouquet of beautiful flowers; there in a bucket of water in the kitchen.'

Emma clapped her hands. 'Okay everyone, now we've all apologised to Marcus how about going into town for lunch? I don't know about you but I'm famished. None of us fancied the stew last night, well who would, and we haven't eaten yet but I know where there's a great restaurant that serves luscious meals so I'll drive. 'You'll come with us won't you Marcus?'

'I'd love to, I'm starving.'

'Ok everyone let's get ready to make this a celebration lunch.'

Chapter Fifteen

Birthmarks

October 2019

Dave and Angela went to their room to freshen up, leaving Emma and Marcus chatting in the lounge. Dave looked over to Angela who was staring out the window.

'Are you okay sweetheart? It is lovely here isn't it, but we do have to go home on Sunday.'

Angela turned round, held up her left hand and pointed to the inside of her wrist. 'Did you see the birthmark on Marcus' left wrist?'

'No I didn't. Why? Lots of people have birthmarks, but it could be a tattoo. Would you fancy me more if I got one?'

Angela laughed. 'No stupid! Although rare, birthmarks can be hereditary you know.'

'Maybe his is genetic then.'

'And passed on in exactly the same place to his daughter?'

Dave stared at Angela. 'What are you saying?'

'When Emma and I were getting changed for our fashion show I saw the same shape birthmark inside her left wrist; admittedly hers is a little lighter and smaller.'

Dave sat down heavily on the bed. 'Oh my God' he exclaimed, 'and no-one has worked that out? That's not possible, surely?'

'Why should anyone have noticed? It's not exactly obvious is it and any mark on a baby would be tiny. Plus, Marcus was in hospital for a few months after the crash and there would have been chaos in this household after Ann died, so no-one would be thinking of checking for matching birthmarks.'

'D'you know Watson, you may well be right! Well spotted. I think I'll take you on as my sidekick after all. What do you say?'

'Is that your idea of a proposal Sherlock?'

Dave got up from the bed and fell back down on it with Angela in his arms. 'If it was, would you say yes and join me?'

'I might just do that Sherlock' Angela whispered before landing a quick kiss on Dave's lips and then jumping up from the bed. 'We should go back; Emma and Marcus will be waiting for us.'

'This has turned out to be a very interesting week '*don't you know*' Watson. Let's go!'

Dave and Angela sat in the back of Emma's dark blue four-door Seat Arona leaving Marcus to sit in the passenger seat. This was a deliberate ploy on their part to give who they now suspect to be father and daughter a chance to continue to talk and get to know each other.

The food in the restaurant was indeed luscious and the views spectacular, adding ambience to the celebratory atmosphere surrounding the family.

It was late afternoon when Marcus left to pick Lars up from hospital. Emma changed her mind about going with him as she and Angela were preparing a light evening meal of omelettes and a variety of colourful, crisp side salads with Lars in mind. They dressed the table with a white cloth, silver cutlery, crystal glasses and two brightly coloured vases holding flowers from the garden.

When Lars came home and entered the dining room he gasped. 'Wow! The table looks lovely; you two ladies have done a wonderful job.'

Emma and Angela hugged Lars, and Emma escorted him to his chair in the lounge to relax until dinner was served. He happily followed her instruction and was quietly laughing at the attention afforded him.

Emma started giggling. 'Dinner will be served in twenty minutes gentlemen!' she hailed, then lowered her voice, 'In the meantime maybe Uncle Dave will serve appropriate aperitifs?'

The mood was set for a very welcoming and emotional family dinner.

Chapter Sixteen

Goodbye

October 2019

Saturday dawned with the prospect of a sunny but humid day for Dave and Angela's last full day in Bergen. They purposely made no specific plans for the day other than to spend time with Lars and Emma.

Emma was already in the kitchen cooking breakfast for Lars who was sitting in the lounge staring out the window. Dave didn't want to disturb him so went to investigate the delicious aromas wafting towards him.

'You're up early Emma.'

'Morning Uncle Dave, that's because I don't want to waste a moment of today. Grandpa's in the lounge.'

'Yes I saw him but thought it best not to disturb him as he's deep in thought.'

'He's upset you're leaving tomorrow.'

'Thank goodness he's got you Emma.'

'I can't always be here, but he'll get stronger and he's a very independent man so he'll be fine. And, anyway, now we've got Marcus PI!'

Dave laughed. 'What?'

'He's our very own Private Investigator!'

'You seem to be getting on well with him. He's not such a bad person after all is he?'

'I've been thinking about things that happened over the years and I reckon I've always been influenced by Ingrid's take on him so haven't given him a chance to show his true character. I like him actually Uncle Dave.'

'I think Lars likes him too.'

'Oh he does, he's always treated him as part of the family and Marcus has never taken advantage of Grandpa. I can see now that's probably something which annoyed Ingrid.'

'Do you think he'll come round more often now Ingrid's gone?'

'I hope so. I don't know what it is about him but I've grown to like him a lot over the past few days. He's sort of shown his true colours and he's so easy to talk to; I wish I hadn't listened to Ingrid.'

Lars heard the chatter and came to investigate. He joined the conversation and it was clear Marcus would always be welcomed by Lars. Dave was conscious of the conversation he and Angela had on birthmarks, but this wasn't the time to bring up the subject, especially in the presence of Emma.

'Can I tempt you and Angela to breakfast waffles Uncle Dave? I've got strawberries and blueberries *and* maple syrup!'

'Sounds delicious Emma thanks. Angela's on her way.'

Lars took his plate of waffles and fruit and, looking directly at Dave, indicated he should follow him. Once in the dining room and there being no sign of Angela, Lars wasted no time in asking Dave if he was going to propose before he left.

'I've already tested the waters and I'm *almost* certain she'll say yes.'

'I'm sad you're leaving but if you get engaged here, in my home, you'll make me a happy old man.'

Dave heard Angela coming up the hall. 'I'd better get back to the kitchen; Angela's here.'

Angela shouted, 'Morning, Lars' as Dave manoeuvred her towards the kitchen.

Lars responded happily. 'Good morning my dear; it's a sad but very special day for us all.'

'I can't believe this is our last full day Emma' Angela said as she gave Emma a hug, 'It's certainly been an eventful week hasn't it?'

'And it's not over yet!' Dave said with a smile.

When the family finally sat together at the dining table Angela asked Emma if she'd go with her into town as she wanted to buy a piece of silver jewellery for her mother.

Emma was delighted and put one hand up to her face, whispering 'I was going to ask if you'd come with me because I'm going to buy a traditional Nordic sweater for Uncle Dave.'

'What are you two whispering about?' Dave asked.

Emma screwed up her face and laughed, 'Wouldn't *you* like to know?'

Emma was thrilled at Angela wanting to buy jewellery, 'You should look for 'Solje and I know exactly which jewellers to visit' she announced excitedly.

Dave laughed, 'What's solya?'

'It's spelt s o l j e and we say sol*ya*; it's our traditional jewellery. It means shiny or sunny, and antique pieces date back hundreds of years and were traditionally worn with our national costume.'

'I'm not looking for an antique piece!' Angela exclaimed, 'that would be too expensive, but I've seen an image of a small and pretty silver pendant and chain I think Mum would like.'

'Whatever piece of Solje you buy it will be perfect for your mother, and the design is said to ward off evil or illness. Oh! And it will ward off trolls according to Norwegian folklore!'

Laughter broke out around the table and it was a while before the family's amusement calmed down as Lars and Emma told many troll folklore tales.

Whilst Emma and Angela shopped, Dave packed.

He'd forgotten he'd brought three Jane Austen books with him and had left them in his suitcase. He sat on the edge of the bed and held each volume in turn, passing his fingers over the leather spines and marbled paper pattern covers. He opened volume one and read the opening passage aloud, "*Emma Woodhouse, handsome, clever and rich, with a comfortable home and happy disposition seemed to unite some of the best blessings of existence and had lived nearly twenty-one years in the world with very little to distress or vex her.*"

Dave sighed, thinking... a*mazing that Grandma brought these books to my attention before any of* *us knew her great-granddaughter existed and now I'm going to pass them on to her namesake...*

He laid the books on the bed and completed his packing as he looked back on the week he'd spent with his newly found family. When his packing was complete Dave retrieved the three books and joined Lars in the lounge.

'Have a pre-lunch tipple with me Son. I'm just about to have one. What have you got there?'

'Thanks I'd like that, but make it a small one; I'm intending to have a few drinks later on.'

Lars laughed, 'yes, me too once you've proposed, eh?'

Dave placed the books on the wooden coffee table before taking the drink from Lars. 'These books' he said pointing to the volumes, 'are extremely rare and probably worth a lot of money. Do you remember Angela saying a book fell from my Grandma's bookcase? Well, it was one of these, then we saw there were three volumes so I brought all of them; I initially thought my sister should have them.'

Lars sat in his chair. 'May I touch one?' he asked.

'Of course you can.'

Lars held the books with reverence. Ann would have loved these; she was an avid reader when she was young and, believe it or not, especially of writers such as Jane Austen and the Bronte sisters.'

Dave's sigh was low and long.

'As there is another Emma in the family I feel they belong to her now. It's almost as though Grandma wanted them to go to Emma; after all why did a book with the title 'Emma' fall from the bookcase when it was full of books?'

'I don't see how your grandmother knew she had a great-granddaughter named after her; she didn't know Emma existed.'

'Well I reckon Grandma must have found out from Ann after she'd passed away. I found a book on spiritualism in her bookcase so Grandma must have been interested in that sort of thing. I think she deliberately knocked that particular book to the floor because she knew Emma was here.'

'Do you really believe that?' Lars asked.

'Honestly Lars, I've never believed in spirits moving things or manoeuvring situations to cause something special to happen, but since Grandma died I really do. You would too if you saw the strange things that happened since I took possession of her chair.'

'Emma will be delighted, and especially as these books are about a young lady of the same name. Why not wait until after dinner to give them to her and, of course, after your proposal to Angela!'

'I'm not sure what to do; do I go down on one knee?'

Lars laughed. 'That's definitely up to you Son. You'll know when the right moment arrives and what to do. I take it you're still happy to have what would have been your mother's engagement ring?'

'I should say so! I've got it here in my pocket.'

'Will it be a short engagement d'you think?'

'I'll leave that up to Angela, but at our age I don't really see a reason to wait.'

'If that's the case why not make it Christmas and come back here for the ceremony? That way Emma and I can be with you.'

'Good idea, and as Angela's father is no longer with us maybe you could give her away?'

'But Angela's mother might want to do that. What did you say her name is?'

'Abigail Thomas.'

Lars whispered the name with reverence, 'Abigail'; I'd love to meet her and if she's anything like her daughter she'll be a joy to know. If you all come over a few days before the wedding I'll be able to get to know her.'

'I'll definitely mention it to Angela. Personally, I think it's an excellent idea.'

Lars was delighted that his home would be filled with the happiness of the wedding of Dave and Angela over the Christmas holiday which was less than two months away.

'You'll have to register with the Norwegian Tax Administration, but don't worry about that I'll sort all that out and send papers to you to sign, and your change of name deed will be recorded on the official register by then so you'll be an Anderson in time for the wedding.'

'Wow! Things are moving fast now Lars, I'm not engaged yet!'

'Easy! That's engagement, change of name, wedding. Perfect! And, I'll pay for everything so no argument please Son; it'll be my wedding present to you and my new daughter-in-law.'

Dave held up his glass to Lars. 'Cheers Dad, you really are amazing!'

'Skål Son.'

Emma had bought Cod for dinner to serve with boiled potatoes and a white peppered sauce. She and Angela dressed the table with a dark blue cloth, white votive candles in pale blue glass holders and small glass jam jars of winter fern and flowers from the garden, all set along the centre with wine glasses and cutlery set for five.

While they waited for dinner the family and Marcus enjoyed drinks and traditional Norwegian pepperkake a crispy gingerbread cookie, and sirupsnipper a diamond shaped cookie with an almond baked into the centre, similar to pepperkake but much sweeter. At the end of dinner Emma served vanilla cheesecake with mixed fruit and cream.

Marcus and Dave insisted the ladies sit in the lounge with Lars and enjoy a relaxing time while they clear away dishes. Lars poured the traditional Norwegian Akvavit into three small tulip-shaped glasses, handed a glass each to Angela and Emma and sat in his chair with his drink.

'Skål ladies' he said as he raised his glass. 'Let's drink to what has been an action-packed week culminating in a beautiful family reunion.'

Angela and Emma raised their glasses with a resounding 'Skål!'

Lars took on a serious expression and put down his glass. 'Emma!' he said, 'let me see your birthmark please.'

Angela was shocked and wondered if Dave had mentioned the matching birthmarks to Lars.

Emma held out her left hand, turning it over to reveal the birthmark on her wrist. She laughed, 'It's still there Grandpa!'

'Did you know my beautiful granddaughter that birthmarks are often hereditary and, although rare, can even be identical on family members?'

'I can't say I've ever thought about it. Why, has Uncle Dave got one?'

Never being a man to mince his words when he decides the time is right to comment, Lars simply stated, 'No, but Marcus does!'

An icy silence cut through the room.

Emma's eyes filled with tears and she looked to Angela for comfort at the same time as Angela put her hand over Emma's and gently squeezed.

'Did you and Uncle Dave know?'

'I did notice but didn't think it my place to say anything, but your Uncle Dave and I spoke about the possibility Marcus might be your father.'

Emma released her hand from Angela's and ran crying to her room. Lars and Angela looked on as the shock of the revelation sank in.

Angela was first to speak. 'I'll go up and make sure she's okay.'

'Do you think I was wrong to tell her?' Lars asked in a shaking whisper.

Angela said nothing but gave Lars a look of compassion and left the room.

Lars held his head in his hands and cried, saying aloud 'I didn't mean to upset you Emma, I just want to make everything right before it's too late.'

Hearing Lars cry and seeing him so upset and alone in the lounge, Dave and Marcus immediately went over to console him asking what had happened. He was inconsolable. Dave left Marcus with Lars and went to his room expecting to find Angela, but the room was empty. He went upstairs and knocked on the door of Emma's room. Angela opened the door.

'What on earth's going on?' Dave asked.

Angela looked behind her to Emma who was lying on her bed sobbing. Angela closed the door behind her and stood with Dave on the landing.

'Did you tell Lars we noticed the matching birthmarks?'

'Of course not!'

'Lars suddenly came out with the fact Marcus has the same birthmark as Emma and she went pale; I thought she was going to faint.'

'Oh my God, but it's not our place to interfere.'

'I think you're wrong there Dave, you're Emma's uncle. Why don't you go downstairs and check Lars is okay, and I'll stay here with Emma.'

'Blimey! I'm not sure I'm cut out for all this. What can *I* do? If Marcus is Emma's father it's something they have to sort out for themselves, surely?'

'I reckon Lars has known all along and that's why he's kept Marcus close, but I can't work out whether or not Marcus knows for sure.'

'Okay I'll go and see what's going on down there.' Dave kissed Angela on the cheek and hugged her. 'I love you, you know' he said as he turned to go downstairs.

There was no sound coming from the lounge. When Dave walked in neither Lars nor Marcus looked up; they were both sitting with their heads bowed. Dave coughed. They both looked up at him.

'Okay' Dave said, 'How do we fix this?'

Silence ensued.

Dave walked over to the window and without turning back he continued, 'Well, one thing's for sure, you can't leave things as they are.'

Still there was silence in the room.

Dave turned round and with an angry voice rarely heard coming from him he shouted, 'Look guys' I'm leaving tomorrow and I really didn't expect this. Yes, it's a shock for everyone, but surely you can see something positive and good here.'

It was Marcus who spoke. 'I've always suspected Emma was my daughter but it was years before I noticed the birthmark on her wrist and by then Ingrid was ensconced here and she kept Emma away from me as much as she could. If it wasn't for Lars setting up a DNA test I'd have gone crazy.'

Marcus put his hand on Lars' shoulder. 'It's been a heavy burden for Lars' he said, 'and I should have been stronger and talked to Emma sooner, but there never seemed to be a right moment.'

Lars wiped his eyes. 'I just want all my family together, after all there's not much sand left in my timer you know.'

Angela and Emma were standing at the open lounge door.

'Trust you Grandpa!' Emma exclaimed, 'you have a profound saying for every situation! Now, who do I hug first, my father or my grandfather?'

Angela walked across to Dave. 'Well done you!' she said.

'I didn't do anything; in fact I was worried I was making matters worse!'

Angela pulled Dave towards her and kissed him. The group hugs relaxed and Lars stood up, cleared his throat and announced he was going to get the Champagne from the fridge. The mood in the room returned to one of joy and Emma took five Champagne glasses from the dresser.

Lars handed the Champagne bottle to Marcus and asked him to open it but said he should wait as there was one more family event to celebrate. He nodded towards Dave.

Dave swallowed hard. Emma, Lars and Marcus looked on with beaming smiles. A confused Angela looked at each of them in turn.

The moment that was passing appeared to stretch beyond its sixty seconds as Dave fumbled in his pocket and went down on one knee in front of Angela who was now sitting in one of the armchairs. Emma put her hands to her face to suppress a happy cry.

'Angela Thomas' Dave croaked, 'will you do me the honour of becoming my wife?'

Dave opened the red velvet box to reveal a beautiful ruby and diamond ring. Angela gasped and gently touched the ring as tears fell from all eyes in the room.

'Yes of course I'll marry you; after all every Sherlock needs a Watson!'

Emma screeched excitedly. 'Who'd have thought in one week I'd get to see my Uncle Dave, have a new Aunt *and* find my Father? Yippee!!'

Dave picked up the three Jane Austen volumes, 'And that's not all Emma' he said as he handed the books to his niece, 'these are for you; a gift from my Grandma, Angela and me. They are rare and precious just like you.'

The shock of such a wonderful and unexpected gift left Emma speechless.

'It's time to open that Champagne Marcus!' Lars called, his voice breaking.

Chapter Seventeen

Back to Cambridge

November 2019

Heavy rain heralded Dave's first day back at work.

He didn't jump out of bed with enthusiasm at the prospect of standing in front of a sea of little faces, but instead reached for his phone and sent a text to Angela: *Morning sweetheart – miss you already! Let me know how you get on today – glad you changed the name – can't wait to see it. Got a meeting after school so won't get to shop today. Love you – Dx*

Angela was already up and dressed when the message pinged on her phone. 'Is that Dave?' her mother asked as she cleared away their breakfast dishes.

'Yes, he says he's got a meeting after work so he won't be going over to the shop. As I'm not officially open I think I'll finish early so should I tell him to come round here for dinner?'

'Of course dear, I didn't get to see much of him yesterday and it'll be good to talk to both of you about your time with Lars. Would you like me to come with you to the shop; maybe I could help?'

'I'd love that Mum, thanks. I've had such a lot of company over the last week I don't really want to be on my own today.'

'I can understand that dear. I'll be ready in two shakes of a lamb's tail!'

Angela returned to her computer with the intention of contacting the company creating the shop's sign, but first she sent a text message to Dave: *So you still think I'm right in calling the business 'Emma's' – you don't think it's a bit twee?* Dave replied immediately: *Yes, and definitely not!*

At dinner that evening Dave and Angela relayed to Abigail the events of the previous week.

'You're away for just *one* week!' Abigail stressed, 'and what happens? Your host almost dies at the hands of his cook who gets arrested for attempted murder, you're told the sister you hoped to meet died years ago and is buried in the garden, then you find you have a niece whose name is the same as your grandmother; you discover matching birthmarks on her and her father who she's actually known all her life as just a family friend and at last they find each other, and if that's not enough you get engaged and Lars is organising and paying for your wedding to take place in Bergen? That was *some* holiday!'

Although smiling, Angela wasn't sure her mother was happy for her or angry, but when Abigail burst into laughter she breathed a sigh of relief and hugged her mother.

Abigail gently pulled away from her daughter, 'I take it I'm invited to your wedding?'

'Of course you are Mum, how could you not be? You'll love Bergen, it's beautiful and you'll like Lars, he's tall and handsome and still has a mop of hair, albeit thinning a little!'

Abigail pushed Angela, 'Get off with you; I'm not interested in men at my age!'

Dave interjected, 'Oh, and there's something else.'

'Oh no, you're not pregnant are you Angela? You're nearly forty!'

Dave and Angela tried very hard not to laugh.

'No Mrs Thomas, I'm changing my name!'

Abigail was visibly shocked and looked to her daughter. 'So you'll be Mrs...?'

'Anderson' was the answer Dave and Angela gave together.

Dave explained that when the DNA result taken the day he arrived in Bergen came back proving Lars was his father, changing his surname to Anderson did seem the right thing to do especially as Lars was so excited. Dave went on to tell Abigail how eager Lars was to change his Will to include him as his son and had his Solicitor at the house within a couple of days.

'In the end' Dave said, 'I decided to give in to Lars and let him loose with all the arrangements. I'm still a bit uneasy at him paying for the wedding but it's obviously making an old man very happy to be alive.'

'Less of the old' Abigail shouted, 'he must only be around my age and I don't consider myself old; don't you know seventy is the new fifty? What about guests? Will you be inviting friends? Where will everyone stay? Will you have a honeymoon? If you do, will I have to leave on my own or will you go back for me?'

'Slow down Mum! And don't worry, if we do go away for a honeymoon you won't be on your own. The house is huge and you'll have your own room of course and Emma lives there too. No doubt Marcus will visit almost every day, and if you want to travel back to England with Pete and Sandy that's entirely up to you but you could stay on; I'm sure Lars wouldn't mind. If we do go away we would of course call on Lars before flying home so you could come back with us then. We're just waiting for the date Lars has been able to arrange for the wedding and then we can all organise flights, and we're thinking of staying with him rather than going on honeymoon; we haven't decided yet. The most important thing is I hope you'll give me away Mum.'

'Oh yes dear, I'd be honoured.'

Angela looked to Dave. 'You *did* say Lars agreed to Pete and Sandy staying at his house?'

'Yes he insisted, and I messaged Pete last night to tell him. He's agreed to be my best man so that's sorted.'

Angela took Pete's number from Dave.

'I'll phone Pete later and ask them over to yours for a curry on Saturday if Sandy's not on a night shift, and then I can ask Sandy to be my maid of honour.'

Abigail's facial expression was one of sadness which worried Angela. 'Are you okay Mum?'

'All this toing and froing is stupid! Why don't you just live together at Dave's house?'

'But I was worried you wouldn't want to be on your own Mum.'

'Don't be silly dear, I've been on my own many times over the years and why should you two be apart when it's obvious you're meant for each other? I'll be fine and after all you're not that far away if I do need you.'

Angela and Dave beamed.

'That's settled then' Abigail announced, 'and I'll even help you pack dear!'

Their first week at home passed very quickly and, compared to Bergen far less dramatically. Once settled in 2 Rosemary Close Angela and Dave relaxed into conjugal bliss and started creating their own family routine.

After work each day Dave drove to Angela's shop, now with the name 'Emma's' emblazoned above its window, and helped with final preparations for its grand opening widely advertised for Saturday 16th November which was also Dave's 42nd birthday.

Abigail took charge of canapés and wine while Angela set up for customers their little surprise gifts wrapped in colourful fabric squares tied with satin ribbon. Dave helped dress the window which represents the front room of a home having framed family photos on one wall, a large piece of colourful cotton material draping over the edge of a wooden table a piece of paper pattern having fallen to the floor, and an armchair positioned directly to the front of the window. Two mannequins dressed in clothes created and made by Angela take pride of place in the window design; a little boy sitting at the feet of a lady reading from a book. The chair she is sitting on is covered in red velvet.

Before leaving the shop the night before its opening Angela, Dave and Abigail stand outside staring at the window, it's content now glowing in the light from a floor lamp.

'You two have done a wonderful job' Abigail said, 'you should be proud of yourselves. Why don't you take a photo for Lars and Emma?'

'Great idea' Dave said as he took out his mobile phone, 'why didn't I think of that?'

Angela and Abigail stood in front of the window, both of them pulling faces for the camera and making out they themselves were comic mannequins. Dave was laughing too and took a number of photos.

'C'mon children, stop messing about now, we could advertise the shop in the Cambridge Evening News with a good picture.'

'Don't include me in this one then' Abigail said. It should just be you Angela. I'll go back in and make sure everywhere's closed up before we set off home.'

'Ok Mum but don't turn off the light for the window.'

Making sure the red chair and mannequins were in full view, Dave had Angela stand to the far left side of the window, stood back to take the sign into shot too and realised there was something missing. 'Where's your wine?' he shouted.

'Oh yes! I'll go in and get some' Angela said, 'and I'll get Mum too.'

Angela managed to persuade her mother to go back outside with her and handed her a glass of wine.

With his phone poised to get a good shot Dave walked backwards into the road. The two women screamed as a Cambridge bus with its horn booming came into view causing Dave to jump and run towards the pavement. He tripped on the kerb and fell forward straight into the women who in turn fell against the window, their glasses of wine flying into the air like projectiles. All three roared with laughter once they realised they were unhurt and began to untangle themselves from each other.

'That was close Dave! Let's try again shall we?' Angela laughed somewhat sarcastically, 'but first I'd better get a dustpan and brush, and Mum maybe you'll fill up two more wine glasses.'

A few minutes later, making certain the road was clear of traffic, Dave moved into position in the road and asked Angela and Abigail to raise their glasses and smile. 'Excellent!' he exclaimed.

The official opening of the workshop itself was on hold until late January due to Angela's unexpected December wedding, and although she worried her decision might cause some clients to cancel rather than rearrange bookings, many were excited for her and turned up for the opening of the shop bringing with them flowers and good wishes.

Chapter Eighteen

Is there anybody there?

November 2019

A dozen cans of Heineken lager greeted Dave as he opened his front door.

'Hi matey, thought you'd like a reminder of your Dutch holiday!'

'I knew you'd bring something connected with Amsterdam' Dave laughed.

'Well, it's the wrong time of year for tulips isn't it?'

'Come on in.'

Sandy gave Angela a bouquet of flowers and a hug. 'It's lovely to see you again, and *look* at your ring! It's beautiful; congratulations.'

'Thanks, it was all a bit of a shock as you can imagine, and an engagement wasn't the only surprise, but we'll tell you about all that over dinner.'

'Mmm, something smells good.'

'I've made a curry' Angela said as she searched in the kitchen for a vase, 'it's one of Jamie Oliver's so it should be good, and there's lots of it because I know how much these guys eat!'

'I'm sorry we didn't get to the opening of your shop but a couple of nurses reported themselves sick and I got called in for a couple of extra nightshifts. It's unusual to have so many staff unwell at the same time; I think there's a particularly nasty virus out there. Anyway, after your busy day I'm surprised you didn't want to cancel tonight.'

'*No way*' Angela stressed, 'I've been looking forward to seeing you and its Dave's birthday too so he'll definitely be glad his best mate's here.'

Pete's voice bellowed from the front room, 'I see your grandmother's chair's still here, has she moved anything since you've been away?'

Dave laughed. 'No, nothing's been moved. I put Grandma's box back in the attic with the photos and notes and I'll take another look after the wedding.'

'I wish she'd do something while we're here; I'd love to witness what d'you call it, a séance?'

'No Pete, that's when people meet to try to speak with the dead, you just want her to move something to prove she's around.'

'Blimey matey, I've just got goose bumps so does that mean she's here now?'

'I doubt it Pete, that'll be your imagination.'

Pete physically jumped up on the spot as a book fell from the bookcase.

'*Bloody Hell*, what was that?' Pete screamed. 'You did that deliberately, didn't you?'

Angela and Sandy ran into the front room and all eyes looked towards the floor in front of the book case.

Dave held up a book. 'How could I magic a book to fall Pete? Grandma's kept her sense of humour that's for sure. Here Pete, maybe you should read this.'

Pete hesitated but did take the book, and speaking in a low shaking voice he read out the title, 'you are psychic, the art of clairvoyant reading and healing. *Shit!* She's definitely here, aren't you worried she sees you when you're having sex?'

'*Pete Mackenzie!*' Sandy exclaimed, 'trust you to bring sex into the conversation. If Emma's here it's because she needs to be, she won't be around all the time watching everything that goes on. What a disgusting thought Pete, you should be ashamed of yourself!'

Pete bowed his head. 'Here Dave put this book back. I definitely won't pooh-pooh ghosts again!'

The room filled with laughter as Pete was seen deliberately giving the red chair a wide berth as he made his way to the settee.

As Dave handed a glass of wine to Sandy he whispered, 'It was actually a Mr Men book that fell, *Mr Birthday*, and the book on psychics was there right in front of me so I had to pick it out for Dave! He's so gullible!'

Sandy laughed, 'good move Dave! He deserved to be duped.'

'Curry's up!' Angela shouted as she placed a steaming bowl of chicken curry in the middle of the dining table along with coconut and cardamom rice, 'it's serve yourself folks so come and get it!'

The atmosphere in the front room of 2 Rosemary Close was one of warmth, joviality and friendship, and as there was so much Dave and Angela had to say about their time in Bergen the evening was still energised at midnight.

'Have you decided on a style for your wedding dress?' Sandy asked.

'I haven't had time to think about that to be honest, but I suppose I'd better get a move on, and I wanted to ask if you'd be my maid of honour.'

'I've never been a bridesmaid or maid of honour, so yes I'd love to, thanks. Will you make your own dress, or would you like company when you're searching the shops?'

'If I had more time I'd probably make my own, but to be honest as I've already been married I don't feel a traditional wedding dress is appropriate so I think I'll spoil myself and buy something I can use again as a special occasion dress. If you fancy a trip into Cambridge next weekend you could definitely help me choose. Mind you, Mum thinks Emma would have kept Sara's wedding dress because she kept her letters from Lars, but I'm not sure Dave would want me to wear it and if it's somewhere in the attic the cloth might be discoloured now, or even disintegrating.'

Dave and Pete overheard the conversation.

'We haven't looked inside the chest in the attic have we?' Dave said excitedly.

Pete was eager to get into Emma's attic to see what was up there and swayed as he tried to stand.

'If I'd known we were going into the attic I'd have brought my ladder, but you can always stand on my shoulders matey!'

'You've had too much to drink Pete' Sandy said laughing, 'and for sure one or both of you will fall, plus I don't fancy spending the rest of the night with you in A&E.'

'We'll be fine, don't you worry Sandy' Dave retorted with a chuckle.

Angela whispered to Sandy, 'Pete doesn't know Dave's fitted a loft ladder and electricity up there, so let's leave them to their adventure into the roof space and we'll get coffee ready shall we?'

The men weren't in the attic any longer than it took to make coffee. They stood back allowing Angela and Sandy to walk in ahead of them. Angela carried a tray of coffee and cups and Dave followed with his arms held straight out in front of him, reverently carrying a white tissue covered dress. Pete followed holding a square, hand-made shell encrusted box.

'Oh my God Angela, that'll be Sara's dress,' Sandy whispered.

Dave laid the dress on the settee.

Her hands visibly shaking, Angela removed the tissue. A chilled air surrounded the group as they gazed on the dress Dave's mother wore at her wedding in 1977. Pete handed the box to Angela; it contained a silver coloured headband encrusted with small, clear crystal beads and what would have been fresh daisies but they'd crumbled to dust.

Angela walked over to Emma's chair in silence; she put the headband back in the box and placed it on the cushioned seat, laying the dress over the box and the back of the chair.

'I'll try it on tomorrow if you want me to Dave it's too late to make a decision tonight.'

Seeing Angela's expression Dave ran his fingers through his hair, inhaled and exhaled deeply.

'D'you know what sweetheart, now I'm looking at Mum's dress I don't think I want you to wear it. We know now she was pregnant with me and that Barry wasn't my father, and worst still we think he deliberately killed her. That's not what you want to remember when you walk down the aisle is it?'

Sandy gently took hold of Angela's hand.

'From what I've heard I'm inclined to agree with Dave. You deserve to enjoy finding your style of wedding outfit which will hold all your own happy memories; and anyway I need something as your maid of honour so we'll have to decide on colours and go wedding shopping won't we?'

'You're both right and I've just had a thought!' Angela exclaimed. 'Dave, would you mind if I kept your mum's dress at the shop? I could put it on a mannequin next time we dress the window, add fresh daisies to the headband and hang that over the mannequin's hand. It would be a novel idea to bring back the styles of the seventies wouldn't it?'

'Good idea sweetheart.'

Pete interrupted with 'Excuse *me*, but if anyone's interested in my opinion you two beauties could walk down the aisle in matching bin bags for all I care.'

The mood having been raised to one of laughter Dave played his Country & Western music collection while the four friends enjoyed coffee and conversation on the forthcoming nuptials. The evening finally came to an end and Dave showed Pete and Sandy to their bedroom, reminding Pete not to worry about Emma because she was probably staying in the front room with her daughter's wedding dress.

'That's a relief!' Pete whispered.

For Pete, Sunday arrived to the aroma of a full English breakfast. 'That smells good matey' he said as he joined Dave in the kitchen.

'Well, you know what they say, after a boozy night what better than a greasy breakfast!'

'That doesn't look greasy; you're quite a good cook aren't you?'

'I've always enjoyed cooking and learned a lot from Grandma, she was a great cook and her lemon meringue pie was to die for!'

'Is Angela up?'

'Yes, she's in the front room; why don't you join her, she's packing up Mum's dress so it doesn't smell of fried bacon.'

Pete joined Angela just as she was holding the dress up in front of her.

'*Jesus!*' Pete protested. 'Phew! For a second there I thought the dress was hovering in the air!'

Angela laughed 'I was only checking there are no holes or splits in the material, and considering its age and storage it's in very good condition.'

After cautiously looking around the room Pete asked if everything was still were it was the night before.

'Actually *no*' Angela said. 'I know we'd all had a lot to drink last night but I'm sure I put the headband back in the box and left the box on the seat. The box was still on the seat but the headband was on top of it this morning and the dress had definitely been moved. I can't work out what Emma might have been trying to say but she was definitely here last night.'

'You don't seem too worried that Dave's grandmother moves things; it's creepy! Do you really want to live here? That'll be three of you not just two.'

'To be honest Pete, although I'm not frightened at what seems to be happening I do hope Emma finds peace and moves on to, well, wherever souls find rest.'

Over breakfast, conversations were primarily on dates in December which could be taken as holiday. Dave's school term Christmas break would allow him a holiday between Saturday 21st December up to and including Sunday 5th January. Sandy was concerned she would need to give plenty of notice to the hospital and felt she should take only a few days off, so Lars coming up quickly with a wedding date was crucial. Pete and Angela could accommodate any date although Pete said he would obviously be led by Sandy's decision.

'We'll be leaving for Amsterdam on the 21st as Angela and I have to be there a few days before the wedding, and we're taking Angela's mum with us.'

Sandy looked across to Angela, 'What about flowers?' Will you be able to choose colours?'

'One of Emma's friends is a florist so she'll order my bouquet and yours as well as a spray for Mum and six buttonhole flowers, and I've suggested white and pale pink or apricot with greenery, but of course a lot depends on what's available in December. I'm confident Emma will do a good job though, she's such a stickler for detail and she wants a photo of my wedding dress.'

'Where's the wedding going to take place, do you know yet?'

'Lars is looking into that but I think it's going to be St Mary's Church, which is one of the oldest buildings in Bergen. I haven't seen it apart from on the Internet but I trust Lars to organise the booking, that is of course provided he gets everything sorted with the Norwegian Tax Administration in time.'

Sandy's eyes widened, 'tax administration!' she exclaimed.

'Yes, I know it sounds odd but that's the department which has to check Dave and I are eligible to get married in Norway, but thank goodness Lars knows so many people to help him get us registered quickly; it normally takes five weeks or so to complete registration. It's not a life or death situation so I'm happy to let him get on with it as I wouldn't know where to begin, and he's so excited he's got something special to organise.'

'Wow! I'm not sure I could be that confident.'

'Lars and Emma make a good team and they're both determined everything will run smoothly, so Dave and I have no choice but to trust them. Wait 'till you meet them you'll see what I mean.'

'We'd better get off. I know I'm scheduled to be off work next weekend so when you decide on a time to meet to wedding-shop text me, you've got my number now.'

Sandy kissed Angela goodbye and called to Pete to stop talking football and leave Dave and Angela to enjoy their Sunday.

Pete, now sitting in the front room with Dave and both leaning over Dave's laptop laughing, said they'd moved on from football and were now having fun discussing their wedding outfits.

Sandy was furious. 'What d'you mean, fun?'

'Well, being best man and having a name like Mackenzie I've decided to wear a kilt in my clan colours! I've looked on the Internet and see the tartan is mostly dark blue and green so Dave's wearing a blue suit with a tartan waistcoat, so you two had better think of colours which won't clash with ours! What d'you think?' he laughed as he turned the laptop screen towards her.

'I think you're still drunk! Come on, let's leave Dave and Angela to some peace and, believe me Pete Mackenzie, you *won't* be wearing a kilt of any colour!'

Chapter Nineteen

Decisions

December 2019

Angela stood back to view Sara's wedding dress, now adorning a dressmaker's dummy in her workshop, happy in the knowledge it would certainly encourage people to look into the shop window as it was both exquisite and totally different to the styles of present day.

Although a fashion designer with more than twenty years experience in the clothing industry, Angela was both apprehensive and confident her business would succeed, a strange combination of emotions she admitted to herself. She advertised 'Emma's' in local newspapers and on flyers as a fashion, textile and interior design sewing school for children, teenagers and adults and was excited to be preparing for her workshop opening in January. Looking through bookings she was pleased to see all of her eight sewing machines would be in use almost every working day throughout the first months of the New Year.

With the walls of the workshop painted a soft white colour and skirting boards and door frames mid-blue, Dave had created a clean and spacious look, the overall effect with each of the worktables holding a white sewing machine and colourful buckets of sewing notions providing an ambience that was calming, clean and encouraging.

Angela walked around her workshop, her hand gently stroking the tables, and when she returned to the front of the room she looked back, happy in the knowledge her workshop was as perfect as she'd imagined.

Her mother's voice broke into Angela's thoughts, 'Do you want another coffee dear?'

'Thanks Mum, I'm on my way down.'

Chatting over coffee in the kitchen at the back of the shop Angela and her mother reminisced and contemplated their futures as so much had changed within a short space of time.

'You've done a lot of business over the past few weeks' Abigail enthused, 'and this is only the beginning!'

'Yes, I have to be honest I didn't think I'd have so many customers, and many of them said they'd be back. I'm really excited, and the bookings for the workshop go right up to the beginning of March.'

'I'm really pleased for you dear you deserve success, and of course you have your wedding to look forward to. So, everything's set for Saturday 28th December?'

'Pete and Sandy are flying out on the 26th and coming back here on the 29th and of course you're coming with us on the 21st so we can have time with Lars before the wedding.'

'Have you got someone looking after the shop while you're away?'

'No, I've decided to put all the designs in the workshop and close. I'm in the process of letting my customers and clients know the shop will be closed while I'm away, and Dave's organised a security firm to check the shop each day so hopefully everything will safe.'

'I'd like to write to Lars to thank him for his generosity, so you must let me have his address.'

'You can always Facetime him or text him you know.'

'Oh no dear, I'm of the old school and writing a letter is how I'd rather communicate, especially as I've never even spoken to the man.'

'You do make me laugh Mum! Of course I'll give you his address.'

The week leading up to the temporary closure of 'Emma's' on 20th December was the busiest Angela had envisaged, to the point her mother was enlisted to welcome customers as they entered the shop and assist in answering any questions they might have.

Between them, Lars and Dave completed all necessary forms to provide permission for the wedding to take place, which gave Emma the paperwork required by the parish priest at St Mary's church.

St Mary's church is the oldest existing building in Bergen and its architectural style places it as having been built between 1130 and 1170. Although ravaged by two great fires in 1198 and 1248 the church has been in continuous use since the early medieval period. Following recent restoration it was reopened in June 2015.

Lars was particularly keen for the marriage of his son and Angela to take place in St Mary's church not only because it's his own parish church but because its architecture is that of a basilica, an architectural feature borrowed from medieval cathedrals and rarely found in a parish church.

Light rain was forecast for the day of the wedding which encouraged Sandy to buy a pale blue coloured wedding umbrella embossed with mid-blue and pewter coloured flowers as her gift to Angela of 'something blue'. The colours of the umbrella complimented Angela's Gina Bacconi Karyn A-line, pewter coloured sequinned dress and jacket perfectly. Sandy chose a pale blue fitted dress with an edge-to-edge navy coloured coat. Abigail couldn't be persuaded to purchase a new outfit as she already had a pale cream coloured dress enhanced with navy swirls and navy jacket ensemble which beautifully complimented the outfits worn by her daughter and Sandy, and which she had worn only once on a previous special occasion.

Dave and Pete bought dark blue suits and matching pewter coloured, silk waistcoats enhanced with silver swirls which complimented Angela's dress, and with their pale cream shirts, silver silk ties and matching pocket handkerchiefs they celebrated what they believed to be their excellent fashion taste by calling in at their local pub for a well deserved drink.

Abigail loaned her daughter the gold Celtic style bracelet her husband had given her on her own wedding day and she intended to gift this to Angela after the wedding.

Dave bought two matching engraved gold wedding rings and, as a gift to his bride, a princess cut diamond solitaire pendant on a fine gold chain with matching stud earrings. Abigail was looking after this gift until she handed it to Angela on the morning of the wedding. Dave bought Sandy a fine gold chain bracelet holding three small diamonds, which again he left in Abigail's safe hands. He took photographs of all the wedding outfits and sent them off to Lars and Emma.

'So what are you wearing Grandpa?' Emma asked as she looked through the photographs.

'As Dave and Pete are wearing dark blue suits, and Abigail's wearing navy I think I'll wear that suit I wore at your graduation; after all I've only worn it once and it's dark navy. Maybe I'll wear a cream coloured shirt instead of white.'

'You and Abigail have similar ideas then Grandpa?'

'Yes, and from her letters I've learned we have a lot of interests in common, plus her letters are so, well, interesting.'

'She's written to you?'

'Yes, we've been writing to each other over the past couple of weeks. She sounds like a really fascinating lady and I'm looking forward to meeting her. We've decided we'll both give Angela away by escorting her down the aisle together; don't you think that's a good idea of mine?'

'Oh Grandpa, do I detect a hint of romance?'

Lars laughed. 'I have to admit I welcome the opportunity to get to know her, even if it is only fleeting.'

'Well, you'll have to make an effort to impress her when she comes here, and walking around in your pj's at eleven o'clock in the morning isn't going to work Grandpa!'

'You cheeky miss' Lars laughed. 'Anyway, talking about romance, what's happening with you and your detective; what's his name?'

'He's absolutely gorgeous and not that much older than me considering his rank. His name is Fredrik, Fredrik Janssen, and we've met up a couple of times but both of us have been so busy lately we haven't really had much of an opportunity to get to know each other properly; you know what I mean I think Grandpa! Meeting up in a coffee bar for lunch or going for a walk in the park when he's got time isn't conducive to getting to know each other well, is it? I must ask Angela if she'd allow him to come to the wedding; that'd be fun!'

Chapter Twenty

Impediment

December 2019

Friday couldn't come soon enough for Dave as his Christmas school week was becoming hectic by the day and his stress level regarding his wedding was heightened, but by Thursday he heard from Lars that all arrangements he and Emma were making in Bergen were now set for the wedding on Saturday 28th December.

Angela was hoping to close the shop early but as her car wasn't in the drive when Dave got home he opened the front door to silence. He'd bought Champagne to celebrate his forthcoming nuptials with his bride-to-be and was disappointed his attempted grand entrance had fallen flat. He texted: *Where are you? I bought Champagne and have put it on ice for later – hope you're not delayed at the shop but maybe you've called in to see Abigail? Love you Dx*

Angela's response was to let him know she was with Abigail going through what she needed to pack, and it was taking longer than she expected as her mother was determined to fill the suitcase to its absolute capacity and weight allowance. She hoped to be home by seven.

Dave was in the shower when the doorbell rang.

'Bugger; hold on I'm on my way' he shouted as he wrapped a towel around his hips.

The towel wasn't quite large enough to provide total coverage but he had no intention of inviting anyone into the house, and to save his blushes he placed his body behind the front door as he opened it.

'*Jenna!*' Dave exclaimed grabbing for the towel as it slipped over his hips.

'What a sight,' Jenna said coarsely.

Dave, still with the door only slightly ajar, managed to cover his manhood sufficiently to compose himself.

'What do you want Jenna? Have you forgotten we're well and truly *finished*?'

'Let me in; I don't want to talk on the doorstep.'

Dave looked beyond Jenna as Angela's car pulled into the drive, and from the look on her face as she stepped out the car Angela was annoyed. 'What are *you* doing here?' she shouted as she walked towards the front door.

Jenna's attitude was malicious.

'*I* need to speak to *Dave* not you!'

'Well, as I live here too you'll also be speaking to me.'

When Angela reached the front door she edged past Jenna and quietly suggested to Dave he should get dressed; then she turned to face Jenna.

'I suppose you'd better come in, but make it quick.'

Once in the front room Jenna looked around and her eyes came to rest on the red chair.

'So you've been persuaded to keep that moth-eaten piece of rubbish? I wouldn't accept that for my antique shop basement bargains never mind my home!' Jenna shivered violently. 'Don't you have heating in this place?'

Dave raced up the hall but slowed down as he reached the front room and, although a little breathless, walked in sedately and looked directly at Jenna.

'What's so important you have to speak to me after all this time?'

'I'm pregnant!'

Angela and Dave stared at each other.

Dave turned towards Jenna. 'Well it's not mine!'

'How do you know that; you can't be sure?

'Because it's December and I left you in August *and* we hadn't had sex for at least a month, maybe even six weeks before then.'

Angela deliberately emphasized staring at Jenna's body, saying 'but you don't look pregnant.'

Jenna screeched '*I am.*'

'If that's the case when is it due?' Angela continued.

'April!'

Dave laughed as he dropped himself into his grandmother's chair.

'I'm pretty good at maths you know; so even if you got pregnant in June, which is definitely the last time we had sex, you'd be six, possibly seven months now and the birth likely to be March! Who are you trying to kid?'

Striding about the room Jenna came to a sudden stop directly in front of Dave, and bending over him shouted, 'I hear you're likely to come into money so don't think you're getting out of paying maintenance for *your* child!'

Dave stood and faced Jenna, their noses almost touching.

'If there was the slightest possibility the child was mine I would definitely be ready to accept responsibility but, bitch, *it's definitely NOT my child*. I take it you've had no luck with Kev or any other mug, so you're trying it on with me!'

Angela stepped closer to Dave putting one hand on his arm and gently pulling him away from Jenna.

Looking Jenna up and down and finally looking her straight in the eyes, Angela quietly said, 'I would say you're no more than three months pregnant, possibly even less as you're not showing the slightest bump.'

Jenna's face contorted and her voice became a piercing scream as she pointed to Dave.

'I'm not leaving until I get an assurance you'll pay up, you bastard!'

Angela and Dave looked at each other, about to laugh at Jenna's histrionics, when Jenna appeared to levitate and fall back, landing heavily and outstretched on the settee, her handbag flying from her hand to the floor. Angela and Dave knew who was responsible for the attack on Jenna but of course she didn't, and her face was ashen as she manoeuvred herself to stand.

'I think it's time you left' Angela said as she retrieved Jenna's handbag and grabbed her arm, frog-marching her to the front door. 'Don't let me see you again you conniving bitch; go back to your lover and squeeze him for money. As they say; we've got your number!'

When Angela returned to the front room Dave was staring into space. 'Grandma's timing's impeccable' she laughed.

'Thanks sweetheart, and thanks Grandma! I thought Jenna was going to faint. But seriously, I'm definitely not the father of Jenna's baby; I hope you believe me. Even though she was supposed to be on the pill I always took my own precautions, and anyway the timing's way out.'

'Dave I know you, and your character is impeccable; why on earth would I believe Jenna? What did Pete say – she was after sharing your inheritance had you sold this place *and* more importantly he said she was *having it off* with Kev; that would've been going on long before you left her in early August. I reckon that's the last we'll see of her so please try to forget what happened here tonight, except of course the levitation, that was an amazing poltergeist stunt your grandmother pulled off.'

Dave hugged Angela. 'You do make me smile sometimes sweetheart.'

Angela gently pushed Dave away.

'Why, what have I said or done that's so funny?'

'You're so correct in your speech and yet you said "she was having it off with Kev" and that's Pete-talk; it sounds odd coming from you, and the way you manhandled Jenna out to the door was a revelation!'

Angela laughed and gave Dave a gentle punch in the shoulder. 'I'm obviously well ensconced in your life then, especially if I'm mirroring your best friend Pete!'

'Our unexpected visitor prevented me from asking how you got on at the shop.'

'Today's been really busy and customers have been saying how, what was it, yes, thought provoking the window display is, so thanks to your inspiration and hard work Mr Wilson, I mean Anderson, the customers have been coming into the shop in their droves!'

Dave picked up the post which he'd already opened and handed it to Angela.

'Take a look at this sweetheart, especially the letter from Emma where she's listed all the arrangements she and Lars have completed. It looks as if all we have to do is turn up.'

Angela sat in the red chair, her smile widening as she read through Emma's list.

Dave turned to head for the kitchen saying, 'I bought a pizza on the way home so I'll pop it in the oven and make us a salad; is that enough do you think?'

There was no answer from Angela. Dave smiled at the look of contentment surrounding her and went off to the kitchen.

Emma's list was lengthy and she noted all official changes too. First on the list was DNA confirmation – ticked. Change of name from Wilson to Anderson – ticked. Tax Admin registration – ticked. St Mary's church – ticked. The list went on, and by the time Angela got to the end, tears of joy were falling.

Dave's phone buzzed on the dining table.

'It's Pete, wishing us a safe journey for tomorrow. It's all coming together; I can hardly believe it, can you?'

'I'm beginning to feel a little shell-shocked to be honest; so much has happened in such a short space of time. Mum's really excited and before today's effort to fill her suitcase she said she's packed, unpacked and packed at least four times this week, except of course for her wedding outfit which she's had hanging on the back of her bedroom door. She did make me giggle when she said she keeps trying it on to make sure her weight hasn't changed and she's so excited that it still fits!'

'I'm glad we're not flying out too early tomorrow, this week's been hectic for both of us and I'm exhausted; shall we have an early night and watch a Netflix movie?'

'Oh that's a shame' Angela laughed, 'and here's me hoping for a practice run of our wedding night!'

Dave jumped up, piled the dishes and took them to the kitchen in silence, returning seconds later holding a bottle of Champagne high above him.

'The Champagne's well cooled and boy am I'm well energised, so grab a couple of glasses Watson and let's go; after all they say practice makes perfect!'

Chapter Twenty-One
Family Ties
December 2019

'Are you ready Mum? The taxi will be here any minute.'

Abigail entered her lounge and gave Angela a twirl. 'What do you think?' she asked as she quickly caught hold of the door handle and steadied herself.

'No offence Mum, but you've really made an effort just to sit on a plane for a couple of hours.'

'I'm not having your future father in law thinking I'm an old has-been so, yes, I'm making a special effort to look good for your sake. A little bit of makeup works wonders for a woman too, and including a boldly coloured silk scarf lifts any outfit.'

Angela laughed, 'really! So you're doing this for me?'

Prompted by the taxi pulling up outside the house Dave turned to Abigail, 'You wouldn't have a walking stick by any chance would you?'

'I've got an old one of my mother's; it's in the shed. Why? Do *you* need it?'

'No, but when Angela had to use a crutch we got preferential treatment at the airport, so if you walk with a stick we might get VIP treatment again.'

'You're a cheeky so-and-so Dave.'

'Just thought I'd ask' Dave said sheepishly.

The airport was busy and Abigail began to question her decision not to bring her mother's old walking stick to garner attention as a disabled older lady, but she soon found solace in seeking out and buying lots of duty free gifts.

In just under two hours flight time Bergen Flesland Airport came into view.

Angela looked across to her mother. 'It doesn't take long to get here does it Mum?'

'I've never had to think about it before today dear, but no it's an easy flight; just a shame it takes almost the same amount of time to get to the airport and book in. How long will it take us to get to where Lars and Emma live and will we get a taxi?'

Dave answered to explain the journey to Lars' home takes less than an hour and that Lars was arranging for Marcus to meet them at the airport.

'Marcus is the one you thought was poisoning Lars and yet he was looking out for him; such a shame he was wrongly accused. I thought we should make it up to him and be extra friendly on this visit so I've bought him a lovely scarf from M&S because it gets really cold here doesn't it, and I thought something from England would be a good gift.'

Angela tried to stifle her laughter.

'That's kind of you Mum, but there's an M&S store in Bergen. Mind you I'm sure he'll be happy you thought of him.'

'Oh, I didn't know that! Silly of me not to realise a store like M&S would be there, but as there is one I'll have to take a look won't I? You know how I love wandering around big stores.'

Marcus greeted Dave with a handshake and a man-hug, and welcomed Angela and Abigail with outstretched arms and loving embraces. 'It's so good to see you again, and to meet you Abigail. Let's get you all in the car before the rain starts again.'

Dave sat next to Marcus and they sounded like long lost friends catching up on events in their respective lives. Marcus was excited to say he and Emma found they had a common interest in music and attended a concert together in Grieg Hall. He told Dave that Grieg Hall, or Grieghallen as it's known in Bergen, was named in honour of the composer Edvard Grieg who served as music director of the Bergen Philharmonic Orchestra.

Abigail interrupted, 'Grieg is one of my favourite composers, and I love Peer Gynt; I remember a school trip to hear the Cambridge Philharmonic Orchestra and that's where I first heard his music.'

'Mum! You continue to amaze me, and I didn't appreciate your love of classical music; you really are a dark horse.'

Marcus half turned from the steering wheel, 'Then I'll take you to Grieghallen Abigail; it'll be my pleasure' he said with obvious pleasure.

'I've only just arrived and have a date with a lovely young man already! How good is *that*?'

Marcus brought the car to a stop in front of the house and opened the rear door for Abigail as Dave assisted Angela from her seat.

The ladies stood together at the bottom of the steps leading up to the front door. 'What a grand design this is' Abigail announced, 'Lars is a very clever man.'

Emma was first out the door to greet everyone; she ran down the steps and threw her arms around Angela.

'I'm so happy to see you again and there's so much to tell you; wait 'till you see the pictures of the flowers I've chosen for you, you'll love them.'

Angela introduced her mother to Emma who had no chance to speak as Emma hugged her tightly before giving her the traditional three kiss welcome.

Abigail stood back and smiled, 'It's lovely to meet you Emma, I've heard so much about you.'

Lars stayed where he was at the top of the steps as everyone started walking towards him.

Once introductions were out of the way and suitcases brought into the hall, Emma asked Angela to help her bring trays of tea and biscuits to the lounge which was now full of lively chatter.

Lars asked Dave to join him in the dining room to go through the many forms and letters that had passed between them in order to obtain permission to marry in the Netherlands. Dave followed having retrieved his own file of papers from his case.

'It's taken a while Son and lots of paperwork, but the certificate of no impediment to enter marriage arrived earlier this week so all's well, and you are of course registered at this address now.'

Dave ran his hands through his hair, 'I must admit when you suggested the wedding take place here I didn't realise its consequences, and I'm amazed and thankful you were able to organise everything in time.'

'That's okay Son, and although you don't know it I checked all these requirements out many years ago when I thought I might be marrying your mother.'

'Of course, and strange as it sounds I feel bad about what happened even though there was nothing I could have done.'

'The main thing is, regardless of the past, look what we have *now*! You know me as your biological father and you have a beautiful niece in Emma.'

'Yes, and if it wasn't for Grandma's red chair and its secrets I would never have found you, and I wouldn't have met up again with Angela. I was amazed at the number of photos and papers Grandma had amassed in her attic, and when Pete and I found Mum's dress in the trunk there was a file on top of the dress with a label on it, but I left it there and I'll take a look when I get back. Angela has the dress on a mannequin in her shop and it will go into the window as a display in the spring.'

'What was written on the label?' Lars asked softly.

'There was only one word – Sara.'

Lars sighed and emptied his file of paperwork to the dining table, as did Dave. Most of the information was necessarily duplicated but it took no more than fifteen minutes to identify the original official letters and certificates identifying the Norwegian government's acceptance of the marriage taking place.

'Everything's in order' Lars announced, 'and it's lucky you're marrying here before the UK officially leaves the European Union, but you must keep these certificates with you on the day to prove your status and permissions that have been given to you.'

Dave counted out the documents, 'I'll give them to Pete as he's my Best Man and he'll be happy to have some responsibility I guess. So, we have the very important certificate of no impediment, our birth certificates, Angela's divorce decree, our own personal declarations and the completed witness forms from Abigail, Pete, you and Emma. Oh, and I'll have to put our passports with these even though you've given me the stamped copies. We may have a couple of witness forms too many but best to make sure we have more than we need.'

'The Civil Registrar has agreed to attend the wedding ceremony at the Church so there's no need for you and Angela to attend the City Office before the church service.'

'Phew! You've done an amazing job Lars; thank you.'

'It's been a pleasure Son. Now, let's tidy these extra papers and join the others for a celebratory drink.'

The atmosphere surrounding the newly formed extended Anderson family was euphoric when Lars and Dave walked into the lounge, the glow from the open fire adding to the cosy scene. Emma and Marcus had been extolling the benefits of living in Bergen, especially at Christmas and visits were already arranged to many of the attractions such as the Christmas Markets and Gingerbread Town with its edible churches, castles and even oil platforms. Emma described this fairytale town as set among mountains, fjords, snow and atmospheric light, which left Abigail in a state of high excitement.

'I feel as though I've been transported to another world!' Abigail exclaimed.

Lars sat next to Abigail, lifted her hand and kissed it. 'You are welcomed into our family and we'll do everything we can to make your stay here memorable.'

'Oh thank you Lars, I must say I'm overwhelmed already.'

'And don't forget' Marcus reminded Abigail, 'we've got a date to visit Grieghallen too.'

Dusk arrived, and so did more rain, but that didn't deter the family from enjoying each other's company and conversation, and it was only then they realised there were suitcases waiting to be unpacked. Lars asked Marcus to help carry the cases to the respective bedrooms, and asked Emma to book a table for six at the Big Horn Steakhouse for seven-thirty.

'Would you mind if I checked with Fredrik if he's free to join us; I'd really appreciate that Grandpa.'

'That's fine by me, but maybe check with the others.'

Dave, Angela and Abigail were more than happy to have Emma's new beau join the family night out, as was Marcus who asked how many cars they were taking.

'No problem' Lars answered, 'I'll organise a minibus taxi so we can all relax and enjoy the evening and I'll have the driver pick you up on the way, and of course take you home later.'

Marcus helped Dave take suitcases to the same bedroom he and Angela shared on their last visit, and Lars took Abigail's suitcase to her room which was at the back of the house overlooking the garden. The room was previously occupied by Ingrid but since her departure Lars had decorators in to totally strip the room of every item which might remind the family of her presence, and it was redecorated in mid-lilac coloured walls above original pale wooden skirting boards and window frames from which hung curtains of a deep yellow colour. All of the furniture originally in that room had been discarded and replaced with more up to date furniture in white and grey.

'What a beautiful room!' Abigail exclaimed. 'It's so calming and peaceful. Thank you for your kind hospitality Lars. I'm definitely going to enjoy my time here.'

'There's an en suite through here, and when you're refreshed and ready for your night out do join the rest of the family in the lounge.'

Abigail almost cried; 'Oh I will do, thank you thank you thank you!'

As rain fell heavily outside the restaurant, the atmosphere within the building was warm, cosy and comfortable ensuring numerous bottles of wine were drunk by the clientele.

It was almost midnight when Lars was informed his taxi had arrived. Emma was a little upset Fredrik had to be dropped off at his apartment because he had an early meeting at his politiebureau on Sunday, but he promised Emma he'd see her before Christmas. As Marcus was leaving the taxi he told Abigail he'd be in touch with details of the concert he was booking and he thanked Lars for including him in his special family night out.

'Might we see you at Church tomorrow?' Lars asked Marcus.

'Yes, I'll be there for eleven o'clock.'

'And you must come over to the house on Christmas Eve and spend Christmas with us; there's still a bedroom free, all be it a small one, so bring a change of clothes and, of course, some presents!'

Marcus laughed, 'of course I will.'

Back at the house Lars asked who would be joining him for Mass at St Mary's Church and everyone said they'd attend. 'Excellent!' he said, 'it will give you the opportunity to see the church before the wedding, and I'll take you in my car

Abigail, so that Emma can drive Dave and Angela.'

'No Grandpa, you don't have to drive' Emma announced, 'your car's bigger than mine so I'll drive yours as three can sit in the back and you can sit in the front with me.'

'Okay, but I'm sitting with Abigail' Lars insisted.

Abigail was surprised at the statement from Lars and hoped that the flush rising to her cheeks would be mistaken for having drunk too much wine at dinner, but Angela noticed and alerted Dave with an elbow nudge to his side.

As the family were moving off to their bedrooms Emma announced she would organise breakfast for eight o'clock.

'Thanks Emma and I'll help' Angela insisted.

Dave's gentle kiss spoke volumes and ignited a fire in Angela she had never before experienced.

The breakfast table was set for five people with a small centrepiece consisting of holly and small, golden coloured baubles. Emma asked Angela to fry bacon and slice cheese while she made pancakes and put them in the oven to keep warm. To add choice to the breakfast pancakes, or pannenkoeken as they are known in the Netherlands, Emma did not fill the pancakes but placed bowls of blueberries, caster sugar, brown sugar and icing sugar on the table, with a plate of cooked crispy bacon and one of thinly sliced cheese.

'Oh my word that looks delicious' Abigail exclaimed.

'Tuck in and enjoy' Angela said as she poured fresh coffee into her mother's breakfast mug.

As Abigail opened her napkin she looked across the table to Dave, 'you might have to drag me away from here you know' she said smiling.

'We've already noticed!' Angela exclaimed with obvious pleasure.

St Mary's Church is a large, grey stone church built from plans drawn by an unknown architect. Its construction is said to have begun in the 1130's and it was completed circa 1180 making it the oldest remaining building in the whole of the city of Bergen.

The church has two towers and three naves and is mainly a Romanesque style church with a little Gothic influence in the eastern part of the choir. There are three wide stone steps leading towards the altar above which there is a large triptych, a triptych being a religious painting in three parts with the central panel larger than the two wings; the wings are hinged together to enable them to be folded over the centre panel and were one of the most popular forms of altarpiece art from the medieval era onwards. Wooden chairs to seat the congregation are set along the side walls of the church.

The sun was shining as Marcus greeted the family.

'God morgen Marcus' Lars called out, 'what a beautiful day this is and I'm so glad you could join us.'

'Morning Lars, yes sunshine at last. How is everyone?'

Dave answered with 'we're all fine thanks Marcus and Abigail's so impressed with the area she doesn't want to leave!'

Abigail moved to slap Dave's arm and he jumped out of her way into the path of Lars who was about to lead his family into the church.

'Will you walk in with me Abigail?' Lars asked.

'Of course' Abigail answered with a sideways glance to Dave.

Marcus and Emma joined Dave and Angela and walked into the church together managing to find four seats directly behind Abigail and Lars.

Dave leaned across to Angela, 'can you believe we're going to be married in this beautiful church?'

'I must say I found it hard to believe Lars had organised everything to run so smoothly in such a short time, but yes now I *can* believe we're having our marriage ceremony in this exquisite church and I'm really excited.'

'Only six days to go and you'll be Mrs Angela Anderson; it has a lovely ring to it don't you think?'

'I do, but shush, Mass is about to begin.'

Emma and Angela were in the process of preparing a light lunch of sliced peppered meats and finely sliced vegetables followed by cinnamon buns and coffee, so Angela took this opportunity to ask about Lars.

'Your Grandpa is looking so much better now; is he completely over his illness.'

Emma smiled, 'I think organising your wedding did the trick, he's been so busy he's not had time to reflect on the drama that was Ingrid, and because he has such an independent streak he just gets on with life. Mind you he won't eat any type of mushroom now!'

'I'm not surprised. Have you been told what's going to happen to Ingrid?'

'Fredrik spoke to Grandpa a few weeks ago and explained the next steps but Grandpa decided to drop all charges against her.'

'What? But she tried to kill him!'

Well, she insisted she just wanted Grandpa to be ill so you and Dave would leave early. She said she wanted Grandpa to herself and hoped that one day they'd get married.'

'That doesn't make sense; Dave may well have stayed on longer *because* his father was ill.'

'Grandpa didn't tell her he'd made plans for him and Uncle Dave to take DNA tests and was arranging for his Solicitor to draw up a change of name deed, so initially she thought you were visiting for just a few days and that's all. I don't think she had any idea what Grandpa had planned.'

'But when she did work out what was happening and the solicitor came here she didn't stop her poisonous mushroom campaign did she? Surely the fact she kept on poisoning Lars shows she was determined to harm him and could well have killed him after just a few more mushroom meals. I can't believe she's not going to be charged with attempted murder.'

'The Police had to let her go when Grandpa insisted the charge against her must be dismissed. He's happy he'll never see her again and so is Marcus, and of course I'm delighted she's gone and to be honest none of us wanted to have to go through the court process.'

Emma and Angela served lunch amidst the family's conversation continuing to cover the Christmas market at Torgallmenningen Square, Gingerbread Town and of course food and drink for the Christmas and wedding celebrations.

Chapter Twenty-Two

Christmas

December 2019

Christmas Day dawned with a smattering of snow on the ground and it was still falling from a snow filled sky as Dave opened his bedroom curtains.

'Come and see how beautiful the garden looks with the trees covered in snow' he called to Angela.

'What time is it?'

'Seven thirty.'

'Really; gosh I slept well.'

The couple stood by the window in silence, locked in an embrace watching the snow fall.

'This is heavenly' Angela whispered.

Dave broke the spell by suggesting they get dressed as he was certain Emma would be cooking breakfast.

'I'm helping her with Christmas dinner. You know, she's very dedicated to Lars and especially to making certain he eats well and goes for walks to gain his strength. We've become very close.'

'And look at what she's done to help you with the wedding flowers and wedding breakfast.'

'She really is a gem. I'm so glad we bought her the diamond and silver daisy pendant and chain, she'll love it and she deserves an extra special present from us for all she's done.'

'It reminded me of Grandma's photo of Mum in her wedding dress wearing the daisy pendant and chain Grandma gave her, and once I'd remembered that, I knew it was the right gift for Emma.'

'Do you know when we exchange presents?'

'I'm not sure but we're going to 11.30 mass so maybe after dinner.'

Dave took a shower first while Angela tidied the bedroom and placed all their Christmas gifts on the bed. All of their gifts were necessarily small due to having to carry them in their luggage.

Whilst convalescing from his poisonous ordeal Lars had taken to writing a crime novel and admitted to Dave he would never have thought writing could be so cathartic, but out of the various pens he had accumulated over the years not one of them was comfortable to write with. That being the case the obvious gift for Lars was a good writing pen so Dave and Angela bought him a Montblanc ballpoint pen together with a leather-bound journal for his novel writing notes.

Abigail said she didn't want a Christmas present but of course Angela and Dave insisted they get her something as gifts would be exchanged and they didn't want her to be left out. So, unknown to Abigail, her daughter bought her a one row cultured pearl necklace with silver clasp and matching pearl stud earrings.

Marcus was the most difficult to buy for but Angela suggested as he loves his classic cars leather driving gloves might be a good idea, so that's what Dave bought for him. Of course Abigail had already bought an M&S scarf for Marcus which she decided to hold over for Christmas.

Following mass the family returned to the house to relax and enjoy their Christmas dinner of roast turkey and vegetables before retiring to the lounge to exchange Christmas gifts. Lars said presents should be opened by the youngest member first, leaving him till last.

'What makes you think I'm younger than you?' Abigail asked.

Lars laughed, 'You can't possibly be older than me; look at you you're no more than sixty!'

At that compliment Abigail almost choked on her wine and everyone laughed kindly at her embarrassment.

Angela and Dave smiled at each other. 'I'm beginning to think your father is falling for my mother!' Angela whispered.

Emma opened her gift from Dave and Angela and gasped. 'I won't wear this 'til your wedding' she said, 'and I'll treasure it forever; thank you so much.' She gave each of them a long and loving hug.

Eventually it was time for Lars to open his gift from Dave and Angela. 'What thoughtful gifts' he exclaimed, 'and they will inspire me to carry on writing my novel as I haven't done much writing lately. Thank you both.' He got up from his chair and embraced his son and future daughter in law and, almost in tears he said he was blessed to have such a loving family.

When gifts were exchanged and charades played, Emma asked Angela to help her in the kitchen. Together they cleared away dinner dishes and set a tray of jenever and Christmas Stollen cake which the family enjoyed throughout the evening while relaxing in conversation.

The next day Dave accompanied Marcus on the drive to the airport to pick up Pete and Sandy.

'Hi matey' Pete shouted when he caught sight of Dave. 'You haven't changed your mind yet then?'

'No I haven't you pillock!' Dave laughed as he gave Pete a man-hug before taking Sandy's case and giving her a hug and a kiss on her cheek.

'It's lovely to see you both' Dave said, and then introduced them to Marcus who insisted on taking Pete's suitcase leaving Pete to carry his and Sandy's garment bags.

Marcus drove out of the airport commenting on Pete and Sandy bringing sunshine to Bergen.

'I didn't expect sunshine' Pete admitted, 'I thought it would be freezing here.'

'It does rain a lot' Marcus said 'today's obviously an exception, but unfortunately it looks as though the rain's back for the wedding on Saturday although I understand it will be a little warmer.'

Pete laid his hand on Dave's shoulder, 'Not to worry; we'll have a great wedding won't we matey?'

Angela saw Marcus pulling into the drive and went out to meet her friends.

Once welcoming hugs were released, Marcus helped take the suitcases into the house where Lars met his guests in the hall.

Dave nudged Pete, 'Be on your best behaviour; Lars is a very respectable man so no swearing! Okay?'

'I won't let you down matey.'

Within a short time Angela, Emma and Sandy were locked in conversation about the wedding while Lars, Marcus, Dave and Pete enjoyed talking football.

Emma excitedly showed Sandy photographs of the design and flowers she'd chosen for the wedding which, necessarily, were changed from the original idea due to the colour of wedding outfits chosen and Angela's decision to incorporate daisies into the design. She took a deep breath.

'You can see Angela's flower stalks are wrapped with hessian as a handle, bound in blue and white satin ribbon with a bow and long tails' Emma announced, 'with white roses, blue disc African daisies and anemone blanda together with lily of the valley and myrtle which form a posy bouquet, and these flowers also form a small nosegay for you Sandy and a corsage for Abigail and me.' She took another deep breath. 'Angela will wear her hair in a chignon below a comb covered with small white daisies, and boutonnieres are made from two white anemone flowers and one lily of the valley spray which should look attractive against navy suits.'

Sandy took a deep breath too, 'Phew Emma that sounds amazing; well done.'

'I can't thank Emma enough' Angela said as she and Sandy hugged her. 'And, she's ordered a beautiful wedding cake which will have small white and blue flowers on the top and on each of the three tiers! She really has been amazing.'

Emma clapped her hands, saying 'I've loved every minute and can't wait for Saturday!'

Dave interrupted the girly excitement to announce a trip to the town's Christmas market. 'We'll be able to get something to eat while we're out too, so are you ready to go?' he asked.

'Give us five minutes' Angela suggested 'and we'll be at the front door with our credit cards at the ready.'

'Sounds exciting' Sandy said as she hurried to her room.

'Oh it is,' Angela shouted after her. 'There's various foods, lots of edible treats and handmade gifts which make unique presents because you wouldn't find them in England, and as the light starts to fade about three o'clock we've got plenty of time to spend money and enjoy the atmosphere. Lights twinkle everywhere when the attractions and market stalls light up in the dark.'

Marcus drove the men into town and Emma took Angela and Sandy armed with their credit cards and anticipation for an afternoon and evening of excitement, laughter, eating and gift buying.

The market stalls didn't disappoint and the group of family and friends thoroughly enjoyed their time together.

Over breakfast the next day Lars suggested that as the sky was expected to be mostly clear with a temperature of 34°F to 37°F it would be a good day to take a trip to Mount Fløyen and enjoy the Fløibanen funicular.

'Excellent idea Grandpa' Emma exclaimed, 'and maybe you wouldn't mind if we ladies explored the shops too.'

'And there'll be no cooking of dinner as we'll take a taxi to town so that everyone can relax before the big day.'

Lars took hold of Abigail's hand and gently kissed it, 'and I want to take you my dear to a jeweller I know in town as I want to buy something for you; you are after all mother of the bride and as Angela is marrying my Son I feel you deserve a special gift from me.' He kissed her hand once more.

Abigail looked stunned. Angela and Dave smiled at each other. Emma looked over to Marcus and grinned, and Pete and Sandy looked wide-eyed at everyone's expressions.

Dave broke what became a silence in the room by suggesting everyone hurry to get ready for their exciting day out.

Chapter Twenty-Three

Mariakirken Church Wedding

28 December 2019

'Our special day is here at last sweetheart,' Dave whispered in Angela's ear as they lay in bed.

'I thought we were supposed not to even see each other before the wedding and here we are sleeping together!'

'Does that really matter in the scheme of things? We're all having breakfast together soon anyway, and then you, Abigail and Sandy can get ready in Abigail's room. Pete's coming in here to get ready.'

The couple hugged and dressed for breakfast, then met with others in the dining room at seven o'clock. As a celebratory reception wedding breakfast was set for two o'clock, Emma prepared a simple breakfast of slices of bread dipped in milk flavoured with eggs and cinnamon and fried on both sides in sizzling butter. She also set out a rye cake spiced with cinnamon, nutmeg, ginger, honey, pepper and cloves which she'd bought the day before at the Christmas market.

After a leisurely breakfast Angela and Sandy helped Emma clear the dishes before taking their showers and meeting in Abigail's room to put their hairdressing and makeup skills to the test, and dress for their very special day.

At twelve thirty Fredrik arrived to join the men in the lounge as the ladies glided in like models on a catwalk; they were greeted with wide eyed attention, compliments, and whistles from Pete.

Lars walked over to Angela and kissed her cheek, 'you look beautiful my dear' he said, 'and he stood back to admire the bevy of beauties, 'I'm overwhelmed at the beauty surrounding me; you all look amazing.'

Dave could barely speak but managed in a croaky voice to agree with Lars, as did Pete, Marcus and Fredrik.

Lars had arranged for three flower adorned cars, one to take Dave, Pete, Marcus and Fredrik, one for Abigail, Emma and Sandy, and one to take him and Angela to the church.

Unknown to the rest of the family Lars had contacted a number of his friends and previous work colleagues to tell them of the wedding and invite them to his home afterwards, as did Emma, and they were already inside the church.

Dave and Pete armed with his file of papers and wedding rings entered the church followed by Marcus and Fredrik; Emma followed and sat next to her beau. Angela, flanked by her mother and Lars walked in with Sandy behind her.

The church atmosphere was charged with emotion as the unexpected wedding guests' eyes focused on the beautiful bride walking with her handsome father in law to be and her attractive mother.

Lars and Abigail kissed Angela on each cheek before sitting together to one side of the altar, giving Angela the opportunity to turn and hand her bouquet to Sandy. Dave stood next to Angela with Pete to his right.

The vicar smiled at the happy couple and took the wedding rings from Pete who then sat next to Marcus.

Again unknown to Angela, Lars had arranged for St Mary's choir to sing during the ceremony and this brought tears to almost everyone's eyes, especially Angela and Abigail as the hymn Ave Maria brought back fond memories of Angela's maternal grandfather insisting Angela stood in front of him to sing what was then his favourite hymn, and she sang it so sweetly at the age of only ten.

Following the service the bride and groom with their witnesses completed the civil ceremony with no hitches; although Pete was prepared with his file of papers should any troublesome questions be raised.

Sandy handed back Angela's bouquet and the group prepared to walk out the church, except that is for Pete who quickly handed the file of papers to Marcus in order that he could exit the church with his camera before the happy couple walked up the aisle. No photographs were allowed within the church and Pete had agreed to take photographs outside.

Before Pete reached the back of the church he saw something shining on the floor. He reached down and picked up a silver chain holding a pendant in the shape of a daisy flower, and as he put it into his jacket pocket he said aloud, 'Thank goodness I didn't step on *that*; it must be Emma's.'

Fortunately the rain held off and Angela didn't have to open the umbrella Sandy had bought her, and Pete thoroughly enjoyed being a David Bailey stand-in snapping every angle of the happy couple and everyone else before Fredrik offered to take over so that Pete could be in a full wedding group photograph.

Back at the house champagne flowed and the chatter of happy voices filled the lounge.

Pete suddenly remembered the pendant and chain he'd picked up in the church and went off to find which chair back he'd thrown his jacket over. He found Angela and Dave chatting with two friends of Lars and apologised for having to interrupt; the friends understood, saying they wanted to speak with Lars and so moved on.

Pete held up the chain and pendant, 'I'm sorry Angela, I forgot to give this to you earlier; is it Emma's d'you think?'

Angela instinctively put one hand to her neckline to touch her own chain and pendant.

'I found it on the floor of the church when I was going outside to take pictures.'

Angela put out her hand to take the jewellery from Pete. She caressed the small daisy pendant as a shocked Dave looked on.

Fredrik, ever the observant detective, saw the expression on Dave's face and walked over to him. 'That's not Emma's; she's still wearing the gift you gave her at Christmas. I saw an elderly lady sitting alone at the back of the church and she left before you. I've checked and she isn't here.'

'What did she look like?' Dave asked Fredrik.

'She had a long grey coat on; it had a black fur collar which she'd pulled up around her neck; she was a little stooped and walked with a limp as she leaned on her walking stick.'

Pete scratched his head, 'I saw her going out the door and tried to catch up thinking at first maybe she'd dropped the necklace and I could give it back to her, but when I got outside she was nowhere to be seen!'

Dave looked back to Fredrik, saying 'Could you see her face?'

'No, she wore a black lace scarf over her head and shoulders and it covered part of her face too.'

'That would be a mantilla' Angela said, 'maybe she was a Spanish lady d'you think?'

'Hard to say as I couldn't see her features and what I could see of her hair, it was grey.'

Angela handed the silver daisy pendant and chain to Dave. His eyes filled with tears. 'It can't be; can it?' he whispered.

Dave thanked Fredrik and asked him to say nothing to Emma or Lars as a daisy pendant is of significance to the family and the identity of the elderly lady is unknown. 'I wouldn't want them to be distracted from enjoying themselves today' he said.

'You can count on me' Fredrik said, 'and if there's anything I can do to help you find the lady, if that's what you want to do, then just let me know.'

Fredrik and Pete walked off to fill their champagne glasses.

'Let's mingle some more' Dave said to his bride as he put the pendant and chain in his trouser pocket 'and don't let this upset you; there's nothing we can do about it and we have a wedding celebration to enjoy.'

Angela and Dave kissed before again joining their guests, determined now to continue to enjoy their special day which, like the Champagne, flowed into the evening with a variety of food and music, culminating in an exciting firework display.

The family set to cleaning away empty champagne bottles, glasses and many empty plates before retiring. Emma and Fredrik were first to go to bed, followed by Abigail.

'What time is your flight?' Dave asked Pete.

'Something after lunch matey, but I'll have to check the exact time with Sandy; why?'

'I was thinking you and Sandy should get some shuteye.'

'You're right; I'll go and tear Sandy away from your wife and Lars.'

The house was silent. Everyone but Dave and Angela were sleeping soundly in their beds. The couple stood in an embrace at the lounge window looking out at trees as rain glistened on empty branches lit up by lights either side of the long drive.

'We should get to bed' Dave suggested.

'I don't think I can sleep; I keep wondering about the necklace and the elderly lady in grey.'

'Well, let's try not to think too deeply on that subject; after all, what can we do? There's probably an explanation, like she often calls into the church and likes to watch weddings. And as to the pendant, any one of the other ladies in the church might have dropped it although no one here said they lost anything, and after all there must be thousands of similar pendants out there.'

'You're right of course, but how come she disappeared?'

'Mmm I don't know the answer to that conundrum but this, sweetheart, is our first night as husband and wife. You're not going to deny me the pleasure of your undivided attention, tonight of all nights are you?'

'I wouldn't do that Mr Anderson.'

'Then lead the way *Mrs* Anderson!'

Chapter Twenty-Four

Love Never Dies

Fredrik left the house before anyone else was out of bed. Lars was in the kitchen making coffee and toast when Dave walked in.

'Good morning Son, I trust you slept well' he said with a grin.

Dave smiled.

'Your friends are leaving today; such a shame they couldn't stay longer, I like them.'

'Thanks for everything you've done for me, and especially Angela, you mean a great deal to us you know.'

'I know Son, you're both very special people and I hope you can come visit me often.'

'I promise we'll visit every school holiday, even if it's only for a few days.'

'Do you think Abigail will come with you; I've grown very fond of her.'

'I've got a feeling she will.'

Pete and Sandy left their packed suitcases and suit bags in the hall and went into the lounge to join Lars and Dave.

'You must have breakfast' Lars insisted, 'I'll put another jug of coffee on and make some toast; will that do for now?'

'I'll help,' Sandy insisted as she followed Lars to the kitchen.

'Are you going to try and find that old lady?' Pete whispered to Dave.

'Whoever she is, she's here and we're going home on Wednesday so there's not much point trying to trace her and, if we did, what would we say, we found your necklace and thought you ought to have it back?'

'But it's what the daisy necklace means to you; surely it can't be a coincidence?'

'Whatever it is I've decided to put it out of my mind – at least for now.'

'Suppose your mother didn't die in the accident and that was her in the church?'

'Impossible! She did die.'

'Then do you think it was your grandmother?'

What! A ghost you mean?'

'Well, the old lady wasn't outside when I opened the church doors and I was right behind her, plus there was absolutely no-one outside with a walking stick. She couldn't have just disappeared. Will you keep the pendant and chain?'

'None of the ladies here last night seem to have lost it and I can't bring myself to throw it away, but don't let's talk about it anymore, Angela's coming in.'

Pete held out his arms to Angela, 'What a fantastic wedding that was, and thank you for making an honest man of this guy' he said as he walked forward and hugged her.

'Put my wife down Pete!' Dave shouted across the room, 'here comes breakfast.'

All too soon breakfast was over. Marcus arrived to take Pete and Sandy to the airport and the happy conversations between friends disappeared too.

Lars looked across to Dave, 'Marcus will come here on Wednesday to take you to the airport. I can hardly believe it's almost time for you to go too.'

Angela whispered to Abigail 'are you going to tell everyone now?'

Abigail coughed. She stood up from her chair and walked towards the window. Everyone in the room stared at her. She turned around to see a row of expectant faces looking directly at her. She coughed again.

'I know I'm an old woman' she said, 'and because of that I can't expect to have many years left so I've made a decision which will affect all of you – well, it might do if my plan comes off.'

'For goodness sake Mum get on with it!'

Dave ran his hands through his hair and turned to Angela, 'Is she okay?'

Angela didn't respond except to smile.

'The fact is' Abigail said boldly, 'I don't want to go back with you!'

An electric shockwave passed through the air.

Lars clapped his hands and smiled as he got up from his chair and walked to the window. He held Abigail's face and kissed her lips gently as every other mouth in the room fell open. He stood beside Abigail and held her hand, saying 'we've decided to spend what's left of our lives together, here in Bergen.'

'And' Abigail added, looking directly at Angela, 'if we find we feel the same way about each other in say, six months, I'll organise a transfer of my house to you and Dave and you can move in and sell the bungalow if that's what you'd like to do. We'll talk about it in a few months but life's too short to put important things on hold for too long.'

Emma couldn't hold back her tears of joy; she ran over to Lars and Abigail and hugged them both. Dave and Angela joined in the long embrace as Emma stepped back a little, screeched with delight and said, 'We'd better make sure we enjoy every minute of each day we've got left to spend together this holiday, and what a fantastic New Year we all have to look forward to!'

A roar of cheers reverberated throughout the lounge followed immediately by a strong blast of cold air swirling and pushing Emma back into the family hug before wrapping itself as an icy sheet around all of them. Its hold released, the cold blast then whooshed loudly through and out the room.

'What was *that?*' Emma screamed with a visible shudder as she left the huddle and hurried across the room, 'the front door must be wide open!'

Dave and Angela looked at each other and smiled.

'Don't worry Emma' Dave called out, 'it was Grandma joining her family for one last spiritual hug to show us she's happy everything's turned out well.'

Emma came back into the lounge, a shocked look on her face.

'The door isn't open Uncle Dave!'

Although a little overwhelmed, the family regrouped into a warm and loving hug.

Dave stood aside and quietly announced, 'Grandma's at peace now and can move on.'

As one, the whole family whispered...

'*Goodbye Grandma.*'

Epilogue

Angela's workshop proved to be an enormous success regardless of the UK corona virus lockdowns during 2020 and 2021, and Abigail remained in Bergen throughout this time.

Although the workshop itself was unable to function during lockdowns, Angela developed an online design course for her clients and this excelled beyond her wildest dreams. The opening introduction to her online classes includes a view of the shop window where the mannequin can be seen standing to one side wearing Sara's 1970's wedding dress and, in the background, the red chair with a book lying open on its cushion seat.

Emma and Fredrik married in 2021 with the minimum of wedding guests and the service was seen by Dave and Angela in Cambridge via Zoom. As travel restrictions were lifted from Saturday February 12 2022, which coincided with Dave's school spring holiday, the couple visited their Bergen family for the first time since their own wedding in 2019.

2 Rosemary Close sold quickly and it was then that Dave cleared the attic and recovered his grandmother's file labelled 'Sara'. The file contained numerous reports from private investigators, letters from local police and copies

of all of Emma's own correspondence. He found no daisy pendant and chain, wedding ring or death certificate for his mother...

Acknowledgements

I am particularly indebted to my friend Sara F who has been a constant support whilst on my journey to complete this story; she is in fact in every sense an inspirational lady.

Thank you to my friends and family who were kind enough to patiently review the first few chapters of this story, giving me encouragement to carry on.

A special thank you goes to Mariakirken Bergen for help with dates and events. I will definitely visit the beautiful St Mary's Church in the near future.

And, last but not least to you the readers for being brave enough to read my first venture into this genre (or these genres!) – I do hope you enjoyed the story.

As there are now many genres in the literary world with numerous sub-categories, this made choosing one particular genre impossible as 'The Old Red Chair and its Secrets' appears to fall into three categories, Women's, Realistic and Romance, with a smattering of supernatural fiction!

I'm happy to admit I simply bonded with my characters as I peeked into their worlds, and I thank them for allowing me to enter their personal lives and tell you what I found. I therefore acknowledge and thank them too.

May is the author of many short stories as well as magazine articles encompassing local village history (Cambridgeshire County Life) and family history (Family Tree); she also produced a cook book with recipes from family and friends.

In conjunction with her Grandson Connor who lives in America and who expertly illustrated all images within and including the front cover of 'Mario Bros', she published (with permission from Nintendo) that special, personalised book for him as a gift on his ninth birthday – he's 23this year!

Following voluntary work with groups of extension readers at a local junior school being curtailed due to Covid-19 lockdown 2020, May missed those children so much she wrote a children's book with the title 'As if by Magic', a story of a group of nine-year-old school friends exploring a nearby wood where magic happens!

A retired OAP, May lives in a Cambridgeshire village in England with her husband, son and handsome Golden Retriever 'H'; her daughter and grandchildren live in America.

* D I D 3 3 8 6 0 2 3 *

L - #0089 - 230922 - C0 - 216/140/13 - PB - DID3386023